Davis

BLOOD BROTHERHOOD BOOK 2

KATHI S. BARTON

World Castle Publishing, LLC
Pensacola, Florida
Copyright © Kathi S. Barton 2015
Hardback ISBN: 9781629892733
Print ISBN: 9781629892740
eBook ISBN: 9781629892757
First Edition World Castle Publishing, LLC June 12, 2015
http://www.worldcastlepublishing.com
Licensing Notes
Cover: Karen Fuller
Editor: Eric Johnston
Editor: Maxine Bringenberg

Chapter 1

His arms ached and his body was spent. Davis wasn't sure, but he thought perhaps he might have liked a nap before getting out of bed today. Laughing to himself, he leaned back against the wall where he had cornered several of the malefactors to kill them and closed his eyes. Sliding down the wall to the ground seemed as natural to him as breathing did. He kept his sword in his hand just in the event one of the malefactors decided he needed to be killed again.

There were only the three of them out trying to save the world...him, Skylar, and Remy. But there were—and he knew this to be fact rather than an exaggeration—millions of the malefactors. Just today Jarvis had told them that at the rate they, the malefactors, were going, they would achieve world domination in about seven months. Not good.

Something hit him in the forehead as he lay there. He didn't care at this point if the entire building fell on him so long as he got a moment's rest. But when a second thing hit him, he opened his eyes to see the woman across from him picking up something else to hit him with.

As soon as she stood up and looked his way, she stood as still as a deer in headlights. Fear might have been in her eyes, but he could see that she was more determined than anything. He wondered what she was doing out this late.

"You aren't dead." Davis shook his head and watched her as she dropped the handful of stones she'd gathered. "What are these?"

Davis looked around. There were perhaps fifty headless malefactors around him. If the woman could see them, then she was either a shifter or she had a bit of magic in herself. Davis looked back at her before answering.

"We call them malefactors. They're trying to take over the world. You can see them?" She nodded. "Would you like to tell me why you were abusing my poor old body?"

"I thought you were dead." She pointed to his left where his sword was still curled within his hand. "I would have come closer to check, but that thing scared me a bit. It's pretty sharp looking."

"It is." He watched her, not sure what to think of her until she turned to leave. "Wait. Where are you going? And for that matter, you should be home, not out on the streets this late."

He knew the moment it came out of his mouth that he'd pissed her off. She went from concerned citizen to pissed-off woman in six seconds flat. And Christ, it was a beautiful sight to behold.

"I'm not a street walker, you imbecile. Did it ever occur to you that I might be getting off work just now? And that it does not include me lying on my back with a dick in one of my orifices?" He opened his mouth to tell her he was sorry when she cut him off. "If you say to me that you are sorry for what you said, I will come over there and remove your head with your own sword. A person cannot assume something like that and think a simple sorry will suffice."

Davis stood up. It was one thing to be reprimanded by a woman, but to be down on his ass while she did it was something altogether different. As soon as he stood up, she backed up until she was pressed against the wall across from him. He didn't feel good about scaring her, but it did make him feel good that she wasn't stupid enough to think he was harmless.

"I'm not going to hurt you." She nodded but didn't move. "I just wanted to apologize to you for my stupidity and to stand while doing so."

"Stay over there." He nodded and stood still. She was afraid of him. And for some reason that saddened Davis. "I'm going to leave you now that I know you're all right. And if you follow me, I'll call the police. Not that I think they'd have any better luck with you than these things did, but you never know. Maybe they'll shoot first."

"You want me dead?" He took a step toward her then, thinking only to show her that he was harmless. But she shied away from him by turning into the wall. "I told you I'd never hurt you. And I'm a man of my word."

The malefactor came around the corner closest to her before she answered him. Not that he'd really asked her a question, but he wanted her not to be afraid of him. As he pulled his sword free of the dirty ally, he moved toward her.

The thing was going to touch her, and Davis knew that if it did she'd be hurt. Their touch nowadays would harm almost as badly as their bite. Several thousand people had died just from that alone, and it was making his job more and more difficult the stronger these things seemed to get.

When he lifted the sword up to remove the monster's head, the woman dropped to the ground. He had no idea if she thought he was going to hurt her or if she'd seen the malefactor. As soon as his sword touched the monster, she screamed.

The fucking thing had touched her.

After killing the malefactor, Davis bent to pick up the woman, who was still screaming. The pain, he knew, was unbearable. But when he was injured it healed quickly, and he had been stung by their venom so many times he was pretty sure he was immune to it.

As he made his way to the car, he held her tightly against him. She fought the pain, he knew, but she got him a couple of times in the mouth. Blood poured from the wound and all he wanted to do was help her. As he put her in the car, Skylar came around the building.

"I'll take her." He snatched her back. The woman was his. Skylar took a step back as well and stared at him. The feeling of…possessiveness was more than the murderous rage he'd felt when killing malefactors. "Davis?"

"I don't know what's going on, but the thought of you touching her is making me want to hurt you. Please just stay back." Skylar nodded. "I have to help her. I know that she's going to be sick, might even die, but I have to help her."

"Okay." Skylar moved in his direction again, this time much slower with her hands behind her back. When she spread out her wings, an impressive sight every time he saw it, she smiled at him. "I can take her back to the house much quicker than you can. And Remy can take you. That way she'll get treatment much faster."

"I don't know." Remy came up beside him, and Davis growled again. Instead of saying anything, Remy moved to

Skylar. "What the fuck is wrong with me? I have never wanted to hurt either of you before."

"I don't know." Skylar moved again, this time taking the woman from him. Just as he reached for her again to take her back, Skylar took to the skies. He looked at Remy, who had been quiet up until now.

"You want me to take you or drive you in the car?" Davis looked at the dark spot in the sky. "Either way is fine with me, but you know that she's already going to be cared for either way."

"Fly, but no funny stuff. I've had a shitty night so far, and you doing those loop-de-loops isn't what I want right now." Remy put his hands around him and held him to his chest. Davis wasn't a homophobe or anything, but the big body pressed to his back was a little disconcerting. But before he could say anything, he was in the air.

Flying with this couple was amazing. They could go up so fast that it made him slightly dizzy, but as soon as they would level out, taking to the route they were going, things settled quickly. The view was outstanding, and the wind rushing over his body was...well, it could make a man forget all his woes for a bit.

He could see the malefactors better from here, of course. They moved in and out of buildings and cars like it was their business. He supposed in a way that it was. It had been four weeks since they'd had the encounter with Benton, and things had gotten much worse than they were before. Not just the number of them, but also how they killed.

"We're not even maintaining them, are we?" Remy said that they weren't. "I don't know how much more we can do by ourselves. We're not even making a dent in them."

"Not to mention they are doubling their efforts to get into the compound." He could see that now. They were just over their home and there were hundreds of the malefactors pushing their way around the boundaries. One adventurous group was building a scaffold to get in, and Davis was a little afraid that it might work. "It won't work either. As soon as they get over the land, they'll be killed. It's like we have a bubble around us."

Davis was glad for that. He needed his place to unwind, and if he had to think about the monsters getting in, he had no idea what he'd do. He was getting very little sleep now. But the work they were doing, it just seemed to be getting them nowhere.

As soon as his feet touched the ground, he took off for the house. The clinic was on the lower levels, so he took the stairs three at a time. Skylar met him at the bottom of the stairs. He might have thought she was going to tell him the woman hadn't made it, but he could hear her screams.

"What do you know about her?" Davis started to go around her, but she sidestepped him. "It's important that you tell me, Davis. She's in bad shape."

"Nothing. She threw a rock at me when she thought I was dead." That sounded horrible, so he rephrased it. "I was resting, and she could see the malefactors that I'd killed. She was curious as to whether or not I was dead and didn't want to come close to me with the sword so readily out."

"She saw them then?" He nodded. "Weston thinks she's not human. I haven't a clue what she is, but I also say she's not human for sure. But you know him. Weston is as tight lipped as you are about things."

"Yes. He has to check and double check things five times." He looked over her shoulder again. "Can I see her now? I need to see her, Skylar, and short of me tossing you across the room to get to her, I'd very much like for you to get out of my way."

Her laughter made him smile, and she moved. As he entered the room where they were all working on her, he nearly stepped out again. They had her arm, where the malefactor had touched her, open all the way from elbow to wrist, trying to stop the poison.

They'd learned that splitting open the flesh, a horrid and painful thing in and of itself, would drain the poison off more quickly. Remy and Skylar were completely immune to the way it affected everyone else, but then they were invincible so far as he could tell.

Davis walked to the gurney and put his hand on her head. He had no idea why he thought it would calm her, but as soon as his fingers touched her, she lay back and quieted down. Davis looked down into the most gorgeous blue eyes he'd ever seen when she looked right at him.

"You're going to be just fine." Her gaze was glazed in pain, but she nodded at him. "Just let them work on you and when they're sure that the poison won't reach your heart, they'll let you go, okay?"

"It hurts." He nodded at her. "My mom. I have to tell her that I'm going to be late. She'll worry so much."

"I'll tell her. What's her name and address?" But she started screaming again, and he looked down at her arm. The blue blister that appeared there was nothing he'd ever seen before, and when she suddenly went quiet, he knew she was dead. Davis felt as if someone had taken his heart right out of his chest and stomped it.

~~~

Skylar sat near the bed and watched the woman. They knew nothing about her other than she'd been in a bad place at a bad time. And that for some reason, Davis would not leave her, unless Skylar or one of the other women were with her. He'd just gone up a few minutes ago to get something to eat and to shower. Skylar leaned forward and put her hand on the woman's chest.

The memories flooded her, not all of them good either. Most of them, as a matter of fact, were horrific, and she wondered why the girl was still alive. The man in her life, whoever he was, was not going to live long if Davis found out about him. Which would be soon if Skylar had anything to say about it.

He hit her nearly daily. And an older woman was in her memories as well. She wondered if that was her mother, but had no way of knowing. The memories were so painful that they were all she could find in the hurt woman's mind. The man had to go was all that she could think of.

Skylar wasn't even sure how he was related to the young woman, but the bastard was a major factor in their lives. Sorting through the memories and thoughts, Skylar found a little bit about the woman.

She was a registered nurse, and she worked at County General. When Skylar focused on her name badge, she could see that her name was Vicki Carver. Making a mental note about the name and workplace, she dug just a little deeper.

The man's name was Randall, and he was her half-brother. Not what she had expected, but very little these days made her pause. The woman, however, was only his stepmother, Margarita, but mother to Vicki. As she went deeper still, she was happy to see that the man had gotten his comeuppance more often than not recently. But not long ago he had knocked Margarita down a flight of stairs and hurt her badly.

"Skylar?" She looked at Davis as she stayed in the girl's mind to keep searching. "Is she going to be all right here? Do I need to go and get her mom?"

Skylar nodded before speaking. "Her mom is in a wheelchair. I can't tell yet if it's permanent, but I doubt it. And she's very independent. There's a man, this woman's half-brother, who is abusive to them both. I'm not sure where he is now. But she's not really afraid of him." Davis sat down as she continued. "You should know that she has no idea that she's not human. I'm not sure what she is, but I have a feeling that whatever it is, she got it from her father, who she has only a passing knowledge of that I can find."

"I'll see to her mom as soon as she wakes up. It might be better if she goes with me, don't you think?" Skylar nodded and leaned back in the chair, taking her hand from the woman. Davis looked at the woman as he continued. "You think she's not going to like me? I want you to know that I've thought this over, and I think she might be something more than just a woman I have rescued."

"She is. I think she might be your mate. But if I were you, I'd take it a little easy with her. She has some major trust issues." He nodded. "Her name is Vicki Carver, and she's a nurse at County. The mother's name is Margarita. Her half-brother is Randall. I don't know his last name, but I can assume that it's Carver as well."

They both looked at her when she moaned. Skylar could have told him the rest, like the fact that she was broke, worried about losing her mom's house, and that she went for days at a time without food just so her mom could eat. But these were things he'd have to learn on his own. Skylar already liked the girl, and hoped that she'd be able to help them. If she could keep Davis calm and happy, that was enough for her.

"The burn...have you ever seen one do that before? Blister up like that into a ball?" Skylar had seen when it happened to Vicki and still shivered when she thought about it. She told Davis that she'd never seen anything like that and hoped never to again. "It was as if her body had rejected the poison and shoved it out." Good description, Skylar thought.

The boil—what Weston called it later—had risen from the girl's arm about three inches. It looked like a large pus-filled burn mark, but it was as brilliant blue as her blood beneath her skin. Before anyone could figure out what to do—if there was anything they could have done for her—it burst, and sprayed the vile-smelling liquid all over the floor. Even then it was like an acid, boiling the wax off the hard surface. Skylar was stunned when Weston gathered some of it up in a glass vial and sealed it.

"No. I'm thinking you're right about it being rejected by her body. Do you suppose that whatever she is, she's able to fight this thing?" Davis said he had no idea. "I hope so. It would be nice to know that someone somewhere can win against this thing."

"Yeah, I was thinking the same thing." He stood up and moved to stand next to the bed. "I'm going to stay with her tonight. So if you need me, this is where I'll be."

Skylar stood up too and moved to the door. Unless they were in deep shit, deeper than they seemed to be now, she wouldn't bother him. Skylar thought the two might need each other, much like she did Remy. She decided to have a talk with Hector. He might have arranged this.

"Not me." Hector paced the room and talked. He did that a lot, she noticed. Worked out his problems by wearing a hole in the floor. "Do you suppose she's his reward? Like you were?"

"I'd not say that to her if I were you. I think she'll be touchier about it than me." She watched him a few minutes more as he paused to pick up a child's book as well as some colored pencils. It seemed that it had been art time before Reuben had gone to bed. "How's Rueben doing?"

The change in his face was almost comical. The man literally lit up. "He's doing fine. Stronger all the time. And now that he can go out of doors with the guard you've set up for him, he's much less restless in here. I've been taking him to see Miss Catherine for study time. It was wonderful to find out that she was a school teacher."

"It was. And she told me that soon he'll be taking on classes that are above her teaching ability. But the guard was necessary, as you know. Now we don't have to worry about him being out where we can't keep an eye on him." She waited for a few moments while he picked up the blocks that were stacked neatly in a castle-looking place. "She's not human. I don't suppose you know what she is."

"I don't. I have been to see her but not to touch her." Hector looked over at her before continuing. "Does it matter to you what she is?"

"No. And I doubt that it does to Davis either, but I am curious as to why the poison reacted like it did. Do you have any idea why that happened?" He shook his head, but for some reason she didn't believe him. Instead of asking him again, she stood up. Hector would tell her one way or another, but right now she was too tired to fight with him about it. "I'm off to bed. If you need anything or think of anything, let me know."

"I will."

As she made her way up the long staircase, she thought about her day. It was longer than she'd thought, but when the alarms went off in the command room, there was no time for beauty rest. She and Remy had a job to do, and she was going to make sure that she gave it her best. She paused outside their room when she heard voices.

"What do you mean, you have no fucking clue? I asked you to watch over them and this is what you give me?" She realized Remy was on the phone and opened the door. He glanced at her but didn't say anything to her as he continued with the person on the phone. "There are seven hundred people in that building, most of whom are small children. If I have to go down there and take care of this on my own, you are going to be one sorry motherfucker."

He put the phone down after ending the call. She was wondering who he'd been talking to and what the hell had him so upset when he moved to the doors to the balcony in their room and threw them open. He stood out there for several minutes before he turned and looked at her.

"I take it someone has shit in your cereal." He laughed but didn't say anything. "I'm thinking that these seven hundred people mean something to you. Any of them by chance coming to help us?"

"Doubtful. And they, as a whole, mean nothing to me. The kids do, but there are very few of them there now. I made sure they were removed a few months ago." She asked him from where. "There is an island off the coast of Hawaii that is in danger of some very violent weather. And as owner of said island, I thought it was important that they were safe. The guy who is helping me with this project is a little slower to react than I would have liked."

"I see. And this island…is it a place you and I could go to—after the weather passes, of course—and have some down time?" He nodded and stood up from the railing. "Remy, I want you to come here and let me undress you."

"Gladly." He moved toward her like a sleek, big cat. She had no idea why she thought of him like that, but it was stuck in her head now, and she could think of nothing else. "Did you know that as of this morning, you own the island too? And all your debt has been paid off?"

"No. I told you not to do that." Not that she cared at this point, but she thought she'd let him think she did. "I got my first pay yesterday. When you said it paid well, I had no idea how well. What am I going to do with so much money?"

The money, mostly in jewels and gems, came in the form of a drop off. There was cash as well, about twenty grand worth. She had no idea how much the other items in it were worth.

And "drop off" was just what had happened. She'd been in the kitchen with Ann, the cook, when the box was suddenly in front of her. She knew that the same thing had happened to Davis, as well as the rest of the people who worked with them. Jarvis had been so surprised by it he had asked her several times if it was a joke.

"I'm sure you'll think of something." Remy was nearly naked by the time he got to her. "Skylar, you are much too dressed for me to make love to you. What would I have to do to get you stripped down and in the bed?"

"Make me come."

His grin should have warned her of something, but all it did was make her entire body get warm. She watched as Remy raised his hand up and put his thumb and finger together as if he were going to snap them. And when he did, Skylar screamed.

The climax didn't just take her but bowled her over, turned her inside out, and then shattered her. As she reached for the bedpost because standing up was no longer an option, he did it again, bringing her to her knees. Before she could beg him—because she was going to beg for all she was worth for him to stop—he did it twice more. Skylar was swallowed up in the darkness before he could do it a fourth time. Christ, the things he could do to her was her last thought for a while.

Chapter 2

Vicki woke quickly. Living in fear of not knowing when someone was going to be standing over you with a fist doubled up, as she had done for the last few years, had taught her that. But the man standing over her, the man dressed almost entirely in white, made her pause before she hit out. He was a doctor, she'd bet her life on it.

"Hello." His smile reached his eyes, but she had no reason to trust that it was a genuine smile, and she backed from him when he moved closer. "I'm checking your vitals. And I've already changed the bandage on your arm. Do you have any pain?"

Her arm. Jerking back from him again, he let her this time. Vicki looked at her arm and then up at him again. This time his smile was huge, like he knew a great secret. She trusted that less than she did the smile.

"Where am I?"

"The clinic."

"Well, that was helpful. Thanks so much. I don't suppose you could enlighten me on how the hell I got here and when I did? I know for a fact that I don't know you, so you're not someone that I have worked with, and the fact that you said clinic and not hospital makes me think this is a private place and not public."

"I can tell you how you got here and when."

Instead of doing either, he sat down in the chair and pulled out a small notepad. She'd seen enough doctors to know this was not ordinary. Most doctors, in the hospital she worked at anyway, had a nurse standby, usually her, to take notes.

When he slipped it into his pocket, she sat up in the bed. "Your name is Vicki Carver, right?"

"It is. And you would be who? And don't think I didn't notice that you didn't tell me where I am. I'd like to know that now. As well as how long I've been here." He stood up again and reached for a chart at the end of her bed and handed it to her. She opened it up to the first page.

"You've been here five days. Well, six days and five nights. This is the clinic that serves this building. There are no nurses here, except for you, of course, and I'm the only doctor. I have help, but none that are qualified to do much but stitch up a wound if need be." He sat down again. "As you can see, you had a nasty burn on your arm. The notes I've put in the margins are mine, but if you have questions about them, just ask. As to how you got here, what do you remember about how you were burned?"

She read over the entire chart before answering him. The information was very detailed, and she was impressed at how clear his hand writing was. Vicki was used to working with doctors who made it their business to write so terribly that you had to call them to see what it said, then listen for ten minutes on the importance of their downtime. Christ, doctors were arrogant assholes. She had a feeling this man was different.

"I was walking home from work—eleven-to-seven shift—when I saw this man in the alley. I had a feeling that he was dead or dying, because of all the…it wasn't really blood, I don't think, but something. There were also a great many bodies around him. All beheaded. Again I assumed by him." The doctor nodded. "I don't suppose you know what they were, do you?"

"I do." She wanted to get up and brain the man. "By the way, my name is Weston Page. I'm a general practitioner, but lately I've done a bit of everything. We're just getting started here."

"And here is where?" She sat up when he grinned again. "You know, your bedside manner sucks. Fucking answer the questions. Where am I? How did I get here? And when the fuck can I go home?"

"On the compound that is keeping you safe. Remy and Skylar are in charge, and before you meet them you should know that only supernaturals can see them in their true light." Frowning at him, she asked him what he meant. "You're not human."

She was still sitting there trying to figure out what he'd actually said to her when a man walked in. Vicki was sure that she'd misheard Weston and nothing more. But for the life of her, she could not think what he'd said to her. When the man walked in, she sat up in the bed higher and caught herself just as she was about to fuss with her hair. Vicki wasn't one to fuss with anything about her appearance.

"Weston said you were awake." Nodding, she watched him turn a chair around and sit on it so that the back was under his arms. "I've been worried about you. I'd also like to go and get your mom and bring her here, too, if you—"

"You stay away from my mom." Her outburst embarrassed her, and she felt her face heat up. "My mom is none of your concern. I...I would like to talk to her, but I don't see a phone."

"I'll have one brought to you. I looked at your bag and didn't see one." She didn't tell him that it was none of his business why she didn't have one, but she had a feeling he knew. "I've sent someone to watch over her. He's not to engage with anyone until he talks to me, but so far she's been safe."

"Safe from what?" He didn't say anything, and she flushed again. "You mean my brother. I see. Well, he's in jail last time I heard. And even if he was out, Mom knows better than to let him in the house. I don't know how you know all this, much less where she is, but thanks. I guess. But if anything happens to her, you're a dead man."

"It's been my experience that a door seldom stops a person who wants in somewhere. And as I said, my guy is there to protect her and not to engage unless she needs him." She knew that for a fact about the door. Randall had broken in several times as if it were nothing at all. "And if you don't mind, I really think she'd be safer here. With you. Not necessarily because of your brother—who is out, by the way—but because of the malefactors."

"What?" He stood up and moved his chair closer. Her body actually seemed to say it wasn't close enough, but she didn't voice her needs. And they were sudden too. "What is...you called those dead men malefactors when I met you, did you? You're the man from the alley. The one with the sword."

"I did and I am, yes. They're the creatures that stalk humans and change them. The one that touched you, it caused a burn to your arm. It was very painful for you, do you remember?" She nodded and shivered at the memory. "I'm sorry to have brought it up. But I was wondering if you could tell me why you can see them when most humans can't."

"I don't understand that any more than the man saying I wasn't human." She wanted him to tell her it was a joke, but he only nodded again. "Is there a rule here that says to say as little as possible until you piss someone off? I've never seen a less helpful bunch of people in my life."

When he stood and towered over her, Vicki realized that she wasn't afraid of him. Not just not afraid, but felt comfortable with him. It was a feeling that she'd not had a lot of experience with. When he ran his finger gently down her check, she rubbed against it. It was the first male contact she'd had that wasn't a fist in a very long time. But when he pulled away, she knew that for some reason getting too close to this man would be trouble.

"You are very lovely." She swallowed hard at the sound of his voice. It was sex and a steak dinner all rolled into one. "I'd like to taste you. Kiss you until you're breathless from it and then start again."

"I don't want you to kiss me." It was a lie and they both knew it. And even as he lowered his head to hers, she protested again, until his mouth touched hers.

It wasn't a kiss. Their lips touched, but that was as far as it was in the realm of kissing. He took from her, gave her as much. His mouth moved over hers in a way that made her think he was memorizing her, becoming a part of her. When he asked for entrance to her mouth with his tongue, Vicki could no more have stopped him than she could have stopped her heart from beating. And it was beating. Hard and at such a fast rate that she put her hand over it to see that it was still in her chest and not pounding its way out. But when his hand moved hers and cupped her breast, she felt as if she'd not just been touched by him but marked with a heat so hot that it took her breath away.

His fingers worked at her nipple, tugging and pulling on it until she wanted to lay back and have him suckle at it. As his mouth moved down her chin, over her throat, there was a small pinch, a feeling that he'd nipped a little too hard, but then he was taking her breast into his mouth.

"Yes." Her cry burned from her throat. He was sucking at her nipple so hard that she curled her fingers into his hair to have him suck harder. She also thought if he stopped now, she would hurt him. The pleasure of it was so intense, so overwhelming that she was close to coming. When he lifted his head from her, Vicki looked into his eyes and nearly came with what she saw there.

Hunger. He was hungry for her, and she wanted him to have his fill. "I want you. I want to take you right here and now. Taste your cum on my mouth while you ride my mouth. Then I want to take you, slide my cock into your heat and fill you with my body. Christ, I want you."

All of that sounded good to her, and she nodded to him. Vicki knew that if she tried to speak, tried to tell him that's just what she wanted too, that it would be garbled and incoherent. When he pushed her back against the pillow and pulled the gown free of her body, she watched his face as he looked at her. Vicki closed her legs when she felt how hot and wet she was.

"Not for me." He pulled her thighs apart and slid his finger into her curls. "So wet. And hot. Christ, I need to drink from you. I want to taste you when you come. I need to drink you down."

It was all she could do not to scream when he buried his face at her pussy. She did cry out when he sucked on her clit and her climax, quick and hard, had her pulling the pillow over her mouth so she'd not bring the house down on them. But he wasn't finished with her and before she knew it, Vicki found herself in his arms and her legs wrapped around him as he took her to the wall across the room. His mouth was buried at her throat. And when he lifted his head, she thought perhaps he was going to devour her right then.

"I'm going to fuck you. It'll be hard, I'm sorry, but I need you." Her back pressed against the wall, and she felt his cock at her entrance. Before she could tell him that she was a virgin, he slammed deep, taking her breath away with both the pain and the pleasure.

He didn't move and neither did she. Vicki wasn't even sure she could, but held him to her as he spoke. What he said didn't really matter, but the fact that she kept hearing him say he was sorry over and over touched her heart deeply. When he finally lifted his head and looked at her, she could see that he was truly sorry, but he was no less hungry for her. Sliding her hips up to get into a more comfortable position brought a low and sexy moan from him.

"You move like that again and all my good intentions of putting you back to bed without finishing this will go out the window." He sounded so gruff that she laughed. "You're making me harder every time you tighten around me. You're so wet that I can feel you on my balls. And Christ woman, you are so tight that sliding inside of you is going to be pure pleasure."

"Like this." She squeezed him hard, feeling his cock move in and out of her as he rolled into her. "That feels wonderful. Do it again."

He complied with her command and kept doing it over and over. He moved slowly, his body holding her still while his hips gave her so much pleasure. When she felt his mouth at her throat, she moved her head enough so that he could kiss her there. The bite—because she was sure that was what it was—brought her to the most explosive climax she'd had so far. And when he ordered her to bite him, it was as natural to her as breathing to take the wrist he offered her to her mouth and bite deeply.

Blood, hot and spicy, filled her mouth. Swallowing when her mouth filled made her need more of him. Not just his taste now, but the man himself. Sucking hard, she drank of him, taking his blood like it was a lifeline. For some reason, and Vicki had no idea why, she thought it was. The man was hers. When he cried out that he was coming, his body pounding her hard enough that she knew the wall was being sorely abused, Vicki came with him, screaming around his wrist even as she licked at the wound she'd created. When he came again, his body pressing against her clit, her sweet spot being touched over and over, Vicki came again and knew that things were never going to be the same.

~~~

Davis was afraid to move. He just knew that as soon as he did this was all going to be gone and the woman in his arms was only going to be a wet dream. A fucking fantastic one, but a dream all the same. When she moaned, Davis lifted his head from her throat and looked at her. Christ, she was the most beautiful creature he'd ever seen. And she was as real as he was.

"I need to get down." He noticed that she didn't look at him, so he pulled her chin around. "I really want to get down please. I want to get back in the bed."

"My name is Davis Brown. I didn't tell you before and I'm sorry for that." She nodded and pulled her chin from him. Davis pulled it back. "Did I hurt you?"

"I don't think so. But I really need to…I never do this. Ever." She flushed when he smiled at her. "Okay, that was stupid because I'm pretty sure you knew that I'd never done this before. But right now I'm embarrassed all to hell, and I'd like to go to the bed please."

Davis lifted her into his arms and cradled her against his chest as he took her to the chair. He wasn't nearly done touching her, and he sat down with her across his lap. When she started to struggle, he held her until she settled. But she was stiff as a board and that had him grinning.

"I'm sorry that I took you like I did. Next time we'll have a bed." Her head started shaking, and he stopped it with a kiss. "There will be a next time, Vicki. You know that as well as I do."

"I know nothing of the kind." When she struggled again, he let her go. It was that or have her unman him. When she was free, she backed from him a few feet, but he watched her. She was not leaving here just yet. Her pause had him looking down at himself. His cock was hard still, and he wanted her. But looking at her naked body had him thinking that she was as needy as he was.

"I would love to have you come over here and ride me." She shook her head but licked her lips. Davis wrapped his hand around his cock and watched her face as he slid his hand up and down his shaft. "Coming inside of you was the best thing that has ever happened to me. And I'd very much like to fuck you with my tongue a bit more as well."

"I don't want that." He knew it for the lie it was. And he was pretty sure she knew it as well. "I don't even want you in here. Where are my clothes?"

His cock was leaking, and he used the thick precum to speed up his hand. When she took a step toward him, Davis leaned back so that he could take her on his lap if she wanted. And Christ, did he ever want that. Her fingers at his crown had him opening his eyes that he'd not realized he'd closed and watch her. The fingers that had taken his juices were headed to her mouth, and he knew a new kind of erotica.

"Ride me." He pulled her closer now, her bare breasts at his mouth. Suckling them one at a time, he felt her weakening. As he pulled her forward again, she put her knees on either side of his hips and sat on his lap. Holding his cock for her, Davis helped her slide over him. He was as deep inside of her as he'd ever been, and Davis thought for sure that if he died right now, he'd be the happiest man in the world.

Her ride was slow. She canted her hips back and forth several times before he pulled her hips forward so that each time she rolled forward her pussy would touch his abdomen. As her fingers held his shoulders, Davis held her hips and helped her get with a rhythm. When she started moaning, her fingers digging deep into his shoulders, Davis watched her face as her pleasure seemed to become a part of her. She was riding him so hard that the chair moved around the room with her movements.

"Come for me. Come on my cock so that I can feed from you again." Her head went back, and he watched her body come alive with her release. She screamed out his name, digging her nails into his back until he felt the blood pour down his shoulders. When she came a second time, screaming loudly, Davis pulled her forward and took her throat.

He knew that she'd come again, twice more as he drank from her deeply. Her tongue at his shoulder made him realize that she was lapping at his blood. Davis cried out again when she sucked at one of the cuts and brought him over the edge when she tightened around him again. Davis held her to him, letting her take her pleasure for a fifth time as he sealed the small wounds at her throat. When she laid her head on his shoulder, holding him to her, Davis didn't move. He was sated for now, but knew that he'd want her again soon. For now he was content to hold her.

"I should tell you that I'm not easy." He nearly laughed but just caught himself. She wasn't easy at all, he could tell that. "And so you know, this will not happen again. We can't keep this up. How are you even keeping this up? Men aren't...they don't usually...I thought men could only come once before they were spent."

"I'm with the right woman." Her snort had him laughing. "You don't think that a man like me could have the right woman? I'm wounded, my dear. Simply wounded."

"You're full of shit is what you are." She sat up and looked at him. Davis had never had a bed partner that was so much fun before. "What is going on in that perverted mind of yours?"

"My dear, you simply do not want to know." The knock at the door had her leaping off him. His cock was still hard so it pained him just enough to make him moan. The look on her face when she looked down at him had him wanting to call out to the person to go away. "I'm fine. Go into the bathroom. I seemed to have torn up your clothing."

As soon as she left him, he manufactured some clothing for himself. It was by far the coolest thing he had as a power. Going to the door when someone knocked again, he was surprised to see Jake there.

"They're making a move on her home, I think, because some idiot is there with a shot gun threatening the woman inside." Jake looked over his shoulder and Davis turned. She'd changed into her street clothes that quickly. The blood on her sleeve made him want to produce something else for her, but he was a little afraid of that right now. "Ma'am. We've been keeping an eye on your house. Someone is there that is—"

"My brother. I have to get to Mom. Now. Do you have a car?" He shook his head, then nodded. "That was certainly helpful. Do you ever just answer something asked of you?"

"Usually. But a car would be too slow." He looked at Jake, who left. "I know of a way to get you there much faster, but you're not going to like it."

"If it saves my mom, I don't care if you sprout wings and fly me there." He grinned. "You don't have wings, do you?"

"No. I don't." He took her hand. "Now, when you talk to Skylar, she's a little like you. Intense, honest, and calls a book a book. So don't be intimidated by her."

"I don't intimidate easy." He nodded as they went up the stairs. Lucky for them both, Remy and Skylar were in the kitchen with Ann. She handed Vicki a glass of tea even before she asked for it.

"Her mother is in trouble. She needs to get there soon." They both stood up and moved to the yard as Davis continued. "I'd like to go as well. I need to make sure that they're all safe."

"Sure. But she goes with Skylar. I'm sure you understand that now." Davis nodded at Remy as they moved to the yard. Well, so much for thinking about easing her into this, Davis thought as Skylar seemed to tense up for what she was about to do. Remy continued speaking as he tried to think how to tell her what was going to happen. "We are happy you're here. And that you're safe. What are you?"

"A woman. Where is the car? I mean, if we're going to get there, we should likely move it now." No one moved when Vicki spoke. "Okay. I'm confused."

Skylar let her wings go, such an impressive sight that he only could stare at her. When Vicki hit him in the chest in her haste to get away from her, he held her tightly to his chest. He could feel her fear.

"She's very strong." Vicki nodded and took another step back into him when Skylar put out her hand. "This is Skylar. I told you I have a better way. And that I didn't have wings. Skylar and Remy do."

"What the hell is this?" The fear now spilled from her mouth. Davis felt sorry for Vicki, but she had to get to her mom. "I want to go to my house. Please. I don't know what's going on, but I have to go. Can you just bring a car around so that we can go? This is…this is just too much."

"I'm sorry, Vicki, but this is a much faster way than a car." Skylar pulled Vicki to her and took to the sky. Both he and Remy stood there watching them until they were out of sight. Davis looked at Remy.

"I'm going to be so fucked up when we get back, aren't I?" He looked at Remy, who spread his wings and put out his hand. The smile on his face made Davis want to hit him. "You're enjoying this a little too much I think."

"Nope. Enjoying this more than you think. She's a hellion, and I'm going to love watching her tame you." He asked him why him. "Because, my dear fellow, she is not going to be tamed, ever. And you know what? I hope you never try."

He was suddenly airborne. The flight this time seemed more urgent than the last time he'd flown with him. And Davis could see that the malefactors had gotten larger; their groups seemed to be less organized, however. He said as much to Remy.

"I think the more they make, the stupider they get. Like inbreeding. I'm not sure that would be the case here, but Weston and I have been talking about it." He pointed at a house surrounded by them. There was a lone police car there as well, but the cop didn't appear to be doing much to take away the man screaming at the house. "Skylar and Vicki are inside. They are having a difficult time talking her mother into leaving with them. I would say that the wings have frightened her."

"Shit." As they landed on the back deck, the man came around the house. As soon as he came up to them, his gun coming up to his shoulder, Davis hit him in the face with his fist. He probably should have checked his power just a little more, but the man had interrupted his getting to know Vicki. Remy was laughing when the back door opened. He shut up when Vicki glared at him.

"He's hurt her." Davis started to move by her and into the house. "He hurt her again, I should say. I can't get her to not let him in the house. This loyalty thing is going to get us killed one of these days, but she…. At least this time she locked him out when he went out to the car to get a gun. She said he was going to kill her."

"She's going to come with us." Vicki looked at Remy, then at Davis. The fear on her face was enough to make him want to pick up the man and hit him again. "Do you have a car? We can drive you both to the compound."

Her look of relief was profound. Instead of going into the house with her, as he should have he supposed, he pulled her out onto the deck and held her. She clung to him as she cried. When he saw Remy enter the house, Davis picked her up in his arms and sat on the chair, the only one on the deck.

"I can't stand him." Davis didn't much care for the bastard either, and he'd not even met him yet. He looked over at the piece of shit still lying on the deck, out cold. "He wanted her to give him my pay check. I have it put into her account because we both live here, and she pays all the bills with it. We're so far behind in everything because of him. And he just doesn't care. What I should say is that he doesn't care what happens to us, so long as he has what he wants."

"I'm sorry. So very sorry." She looked up at him, and Davis knew for as long as he lived—and according to Hector, that was going to be pretty much forever—he'd never forget the moment he fell in love with her.

"Can we stay at your house? Just until...for a little while. I won't be a problem, and my mom is a nurse too. I...I lost my job apparently, because I was a no-call/no-show for four days. But we're going to lose everything anyway. Randall taking my paycheck wouldn't have made that much of a difference in the long scheme of things. We were set to be tossed out of here soon anyway, and the heat has been off for a couple months too."

"Yes. Just pack what you want. We'll send a truck for the rest. There's plenty of room." At least he hoped so.

Skylar came out of the house then, and he told her the plan. "We can't let them stay here. He'll come back over and over. I'd like to take them to the compound, please? If not, then...then I'll have to move in with them until I know that they'll be safe."

"Your mom is packing her things now to come with us. You should as well. I'd like a word with Davis for a moment. Then he'll come and help you." Remy came out of the house too, and Vicki stood up as Skylar continued. "He won't be long."

As soon as she went in the house, Remy leaned against the wall and smiled as he spoke. "She's a faerie. And not just any kind of faerie, but a life one. Not entirely sure what that is yet, but her mom will talk to you later. She's been afraid that someone would find out, and now that we're here...for some reason she trusts us."

Davis wondered if there was more. Then something occurred to him. "She doesn't know. She thinks she's human, and no one ever told her differently."

"Her mom said she was afraid if her brother or father had found out, he might have...he would have hurt her." Davis stood up when Remy continued, nodding to the man lying on the deck. "He knows now. That's why he came here today. He has it in his head that he's going to take her and use her somehow."

Nodding, Davis went into the house. A faerie. He didn't even have a clue what that might mean for the two of them. Going into her room, he was humbled at how sparse it was. In fact, the entire house looked like it had the barest of necessities and nothing more. Not even a television graced the living room. And the lamp, a lone one, sat on the floor rather than on an end table. He asked her what was going and was told that only the shirts on their backs belonged to them, along with a few personal things. Davis was going to have a lot of explaining to do when they got back to the compound, and a great deal of it was going to piss her off, he just knew it. And for some reason, he was actually looking forward to her temper again.

Chapter 3

Master limped around the cave. He wasn't happy with his current living quarters, but he knew that he was safest here. Who would have thought that something so mundane would hurt him so badly? The gun, it turned out, was his own worst enemy.

That bitch. She'd done this to him. He was going to kill them all but make her suffer the most. His plan was now on hold; his people, his monsters were awaiting a leader. And he was hiding in a hole so that he could mend himself. Things could not have been any worse, he thought.

Looking down at his belly, he wondered if he should chance another shift. The last time had nearly put him out for a week, but he'd been healed…some, anyway. But he had things to do. Master had to get things rolling again before someone else was given his domain. And he had no doubt that they would if he didn't show up soon.

"There you are." He turned to look at the man. Master hadn't talked to him a lot over the past few weeks since he'd been hiding out, but when he did, it was never face to face but like now, with he and Master in different locations and using a hologram kind of system. "I've been searching for you. When do you think you'll be able to get back to work? The soldiers are at a loss without guidance. While we have a great many of the soldiers now, they are fumbling around and not doing a good job."

"I'm nearly back to my old self. Just this morning I was able to fly to the compound and back to see what was progressing." Lies, all of it. But the stupid man didn't seem to know it. As he bopped his head up and down, Master wanted to rip it from his body. "Have you been able to get me more stones? They're taking them now and not returning them to me. I cannot believe the nerve of them, taking what does not belong to them. But when I'm ready, I will kill them in a way that will have them know that I am pissed."

"We'd like that as well, very much so. Dolin is still…he is grieving hard for Mary. I told you they killed her, did I not?" Master nodded. He had loved the woman as well. She had treated him as an equal, not as something that was only good for killing. "I have set aside my grief in order to get her needs met and her death avenged. Once we have taken over this world, we'll be able to make a garden in her name. Someplace we can go to and think of her."

He wanted to tell him it was a waste of time. Mary would have no more liked to garden than he would. But Master only nodded. As the man stood there, no doubt thinking of the garden and the expense he was going to use to get it completed, Master reminded him again of what he wanted.

"The stones? Have you any?" Master continued when he got no response. "Without them I cannot control the few that I need. And their power once they are given the boost is a great deal of help to me as well."

"You will have to make do with the ones that will be brought to you today. There are no more. I am not telling you this to anger you, but giving you the truth. Rembrandt and his soldiers are making it difficult to even get one, much less the number that you requested. It's as if they are trying to stop our plan." Master wanted to tell him of course Rembrandt was trying to stop them. It was what he was made for. But Master said nothing. The man was beyond stupid at times.

"That man must go. And his mate. Together they are most powerful, and have been keeping me from my tasks for far too long. Killing them will be a great pleasure."

Master shivered slightly when he thought of the woman. She had been relentless in her pursuit to hurt him. She might have even wanted him dead. There was no reason for it that he could see. Had she just let him kill Rembrandt, things would have been where they should have been by now, instead of being so far behind that he was going to be forever catching up. He thought of something else and looked at the man.

"Did you find out what I needed regarding the woman? She is going to be Rembrandt's downfall. But without something to lure her away, I don't know what to do."

Ward seemed to be talking to someone on his end, and when he looked at Master, he had to repeat his question. "There is little to nothing about her. Perhaps she isn't human." Master wanted to pop the man in the head. Well, of course she wasn't human. She had wings, fought like a warrior, and was loyal to Rembrandt more than anyone he'd ever known. "I have my best men looking into it. But perhaps you could go and get her yourself. There is much going on with our end. Making as many of the soldiers as we can is hard work. And with all the people we were using now…well, we've had to start anew, as you know. The lab we were using was no longer safe. It was important that we were safe."

"Yes. I can see where you'd need to be as safe as can be." Master turned away from Ward so that he'd not see his anger. He wanted to kill them all. Simply rid himself of their constant whining and take over the world himself. But he had no contacts when it came to the selling of the stones, and he had learned long ago that money is very helpful when taking over a realm. "I shall go out to try and get her today. Please let me know when you have found out anything as soon as possible. The more I know the easier it will be for me to capture her."

"One other thing." Master turned to him again. The man was looking very puffed up about something. "You're not in charge here. I know you think you are, and while we appreciate all that you have done, you are not in charge unless I say so. And I don't. Nor will I. Dolin might not be himself right now, but when this is over, he will be running this realm with me. We'll have use of you, of course, but you'll not rule."

"You said that I would be ruler." Ward smiled. It wasn't a smile that he'd ever seen on the man before. This one said that he was going to fuck him in any way he could. "I see. Yet you want me to continue on as if I would be in charge."

"If you want to live you will." In seconds, less really, the man disappeared. Master stood there for several more wondering what the hell he was supposed to do now. He'd been ready to rule, not…. He was only going to be a soldier. At best he would be an adherent. That just would not do.

Master went to the opening of his cave. He had to get Rembrandt or the woman. Not necessarily to kill him right away, but at least get to him. He wanted the man to know who he was. Master smiled at the memory.

He had been hiding among the dead when the war was nearly over. He'd been terrified if he was truthful about his feelings. Master had watched as the soldiers, the ones he knew now as his minions, had gone from man to man, changing them into what they were now.

Augustus Benton Hill had been one of Remy's best friends before going to war, at least as far as Remy was concerned. What Benton really wanted, and still did, was whatever Remy had, and that included his wife and children. Killing them, all of them, had been his greatest accomplishment in his entire life. And seeing him grieve, his heart broken by the sight of his family laying there, had nearly made him dance with joy.

He had known that Remy was off to war. He had been to his home for dinner the night before and had been told. There had been much sadness in the house. The younger children had been put to bed with promises of being woken before their father left them. Remy held his wife, huge with his next children, on his lap as he talked about the money that he'd be sending home each month.

"It will put a new roof on the barn and buy us a cow for the winter. Seed enough to get us through to the next year, and plenty left over for a treat for my family." He rubbed the big belly of his wife, and she smacked at him. Master had watched with hatred in his heart. He knew it was unfair of him to want only because it belonged to another, but he did. It was the way he'd been his entire life, and it had paid him well, he thought.

Two days later, just after Remy had left them, Master had gone to the house to see if there was any way that she'd lay with him. At first he thought she was thinking it over, and when she tried to shut the door in his face, telling him to go away, he thought she was being coy. She had been so upset with him, so mad that she'd told him that she was going to tell Remy as soon as he returned. That would not do.

Master had killed them all the following day, bringing with him a group of men to help him. The payment was they could have the wife as many times as they wished, so long as he'd be first. The children too if they wanted, but Master wanted only the wife of his enemy. Most of them eagerly went with him. A couple had said no. They wanted no part of killing the family of a man as great as Remy.

But the children had been missing that day. He had not been able to find them until sometime later when he walked over their graves. It was then that he realized that they'd been hidden from him and his men. To this day it pissed him off to no end to know that Remy's wife, even in her death, had not told him where they were. He'd pissed on her grave and those of the children. To him, they should have been his as much as the woman had been.

Master had then set the house on fire. The barn too, with all the prized horses in it that Remy had trained himself. There was hay aplenty, even some fertilizer and a few seeds. Everything went up in smoke, and Master watched it all with a huge smile on his face. Then he'd gone to the field to tell his friend.

Remy had grieved for days, weeks it seemed. Remy never left the burned property long enough to do more than bury the dead. When he was not at the site where their home had been, he could be found in the small cemetery laying upon their graves, crying and talking to them. Three days after a big storm had come though, Remy told Master that he was headed out to the war.

"I shall not return." Master started to ask him why not. "If possible I will kill as many of the enemy as I can, but I shall let them do their worst to me. I have no reason to live. You should take my land. It is good earth and holds a seed in her belly, and will spew forth a great crop. But I have no more desire to live and cannot kill myself no matter how hard I think about it. War will suit me fine."

"You must live. I have things to tell you." Remy had walked away, and no matter how hard he tried to get Remy to stay and let Master tell him what he'd done, the man kept walking. Master had it in his head to tell him face to face, see the look in his eyes as he told him. But Remy would not still for him. It had vexed him so badly that he'd gone back to the smallish cemetery and kicked over the stones Remy had made that marked their graves.

And that was how Master had ended up on the field that day. Death and carnage was all around them. He watched the man he'd hated for more years than he'd liked him. Remy fought like a man who had no cares, had no reason to live. Which, Master thought, he really didn't.

Then the man in black had appeared before Remy, talking to him and then taking the pike from his body. Master watched, and again wanted what Remy had. He watched, buried beneath a man who'd had his head removed, while Remy was offered the world. And he saw Remy healed. But before he could run forth, show them that he too was worthy, one of the adherents came to him and changed him. Master knew the real meaning of new life.

As he made his way back into his cave, his memories giving him some respite after the talk with Ward, he noticed a box laying on the stone he used as a table. Within it were two dozen stones, all them glowing a bright blue. Smiling, he lifted one up to the only light in the dark cave and looked at its properties. This one…this one with the red and gold in it with the blue streak, was going to be his.

Taking it to his heart, he put it over the cold stone that was already there. It spilled from his body and the new one was absorbed into the empty place. The change, the power, the feeling was immediate. He felt better than he had for a long while. Stretching his wings, he knew that he'd never use the other stones for the new adherents. They were for him, and for his fight against Remy. If this was all he was to have, then he needed them much more than he needed subjects to order around.

"He will be mine, and that bitch of a woman will suffer greatly before I finish with her." Master took to the sky. His wings, still a little tender, spread out and he could see how tattered they were. No matter. Soon—very soon—Remy would be dead and his army would be ready. Master was going to be ruler of this world.

~~~

Remy wasn't sure this was going to work. There were too many of them in one room, first of all, and that would upset the young woman. Then there was the added fact that her own mother was terrified of telling her the truth.

As soon as Vicki entered, Remy stood up.

"What's going on?" Davis led her to a chair and sat down beside her. She looked at Remy, the only one still standing, when she continued. "I'm in trouble for something, or are you telling me bad news?"

"Both." She nodded and looked at her mom as Remy continued. "She has plenty to tell you, but I should like to start. There are things going on here, just outside of here, which are going to come to a head soon. So the more we are level-headed and working together, the sooner we'll be able to take care of the humans in this world. That being said, do you have any questions that I might be able to answer for you before we begin?"

"Yes. Lots, but for now...for now I'm going to ask them as they seem to be important to me. The soldiers and adherents are what you're talking about, right?" Remy nodded. "I don't have a clue what that has to do with me, but then I'm thinking you do. So if you don't mind, I'd like for you to say whatever you think I need to hear so I can go out and find a job."

Weston stood up. "I have one for you. And your mother. We have the funds to pay you both well. I've need of help. There aren't a lot of humans here yet, but the few that are coming in have been hurt. Not as badly as you were, but hurt all the same. I would like to offer you a job. Both of you."

"A job doing what?" He told her as his nurse. "I'll have to think about it. My mom and I will talk it over and we'll get back to you. I don't...there is a lot going on right now, and I'm still trying to sort it out. And I need a job and money. We can't live here forever, and we'll need...we'll need a start."

"Which brings me to the next point." Remy took a deep breath. "You and Davis are a couple now. And I'm not sure why you've not been marked accordingly or even if you will be, but you will live as long as you'd —"

"Marked? As in the way you two are? The way Davis is marked?" Remy nodded. "No thanks. I don't want to be inked. I've seen a lot of infections come in to the hospital because some idiots thought it would be cool to have their girlfriends or boyfriends tatted on their skins. Not for me."

"You might not have any say in it." When she stood up, he crossed his arms over his chest. He wasn't afraid of the young woman, but she was Davis's mate. "There are things, as I have said many times now, that you might not be aware of."

"Like the wings? Or is it the fact that those things, those blue things, hurt with a touch?" She mimicked him in stance and he had to hide a smile. "I'm not afraid of you, buddy. You might be bigger than me and a little older, but I don't fight fair."

"I'm nearly nineteen hundred years old." She stared at him open mouthed. "And the ink, as you call it, was put on me when I was turned into what I am. I have no idea what that is, but we call ourselves warriors. I can eat food, though I prefer blood…Davis can eat as well, but he can live off either. Skylar is my partner, my bed mate, as well as my equal. In all things. And as you are mated to Davis, we'll have to wait and see what powers you have now and what you will gain as this goes on."

"Goes on? I have no idea what that means, but I get the feeling you have no clue either. As for Davis? That's not…we're working on that. To be honest, I have no idea why I'm so attached to him, but…." She looked at her mom when she cleared her throat. "You and I are going to be fine, Mom. We'll find us a place to stay, and Randy won't bother us again. We'll have to work better at keeping him out of the house, but we'll be—"

"I'm not your mom. Not in the truest sense of the word. I raised you from an infant, but I never gave birth to you. And your father, the man that I was married to after you came to me, he wasn't your dad either. He never knew about where you came from, which was a good thing, I suppose, once I figured out that he was as bad as his son.

But I'm not your mom." Margarita held out an envelope. "This came with you when they brought you to me. I was told to save it for you, that you'd need it someday."

Vicki stared at it but didn't take it. When her mom moved toward her, Vicki stood up and backed from her when she tried to hand it to her. Remy had read it. He didn't understand the words on the sheets of very heavy paper, but he did know that she would. He had no idea how he knew this, but knew that Vicki would understand every word written in the strange language.

"They were my neighbors. Not really very friendly, but they seldom bothered me or I them, only to say hi when one or the other was in the yard. I knew that they were expecting a baby. I had seen the woman in the yard. The man was a nice enough man and would come over to help me when he was home. I was alone back then, and he was kind to me. They both were, I guess." Margarita moved closer as she continued. "Then one night I was in bed when there was this horrible scream. I went down the stairs, and really quietly like I opened the door and saw them. I heard voices in their yard, loud and mean sounding, and closed the door when I got scared. When they knocked, pounded really, I was almost not going to answer it. Then I saw her, your mother, and opened the door all the way. She held you up to me, and I could see that she was covered in blood. I brought you into the house, and the woman gave me the letter and left you with me. She said that you'd need it someday."

"No. You said I was yours." Vicki backed from her again, but this time Davis stopped her. Vicki looked up at him. "You knew about this? You knew they were going to lie to me and you brought me here to hear them?"

"It's no lie." She turned on him so quickly that Remy had to hold her back with his hands. "Listen to us. This is no lie. We're trying to tell you that you're not human, but a faerie."

Vicki stilled, the look on her face a study in fear and disbelief. When he nodded, she shook her head and started to laugh. Not a humorous sounding one, but one he'd heard before...when men were at their end.

"A faerie? You expect me to believe that my entire life has been a lie, and that I'm not only not her child but that of a couple of fictional creatures that you know aren't real?" Weston stood up. He had said that he'd shift to convince her, and when he did she stared at him for several seconds before looking back at Remy. The big wolf didn't move when she started to reach out to him, but she turned to him at the last second. "You're next, right? You've gotten some sort of movie thing going on that makes me think that's what he did. And now you're going to turn into what...a large bird of prey that will swoop over my head and make a believer of me?"

Weston came to her and nipped gently at her hand. The way she jerked from him made Remy think that she'd been hurt, but there was no mark on her. Still, she stared at him. He told her to read the letter.

Vicki snatched the letter from her mom and sat down. She opened it with her fingers across the broken seal. He had no idea who would have done that first reading, but he was sure that it was her mother, Margarita. Vicki looked as if she was reading it when she looked at him again.

"It says that I'm a child of life faeries. That my parents were outcasts for their entire life because they wanted things to be different for their children. It says that if I'm reading this...." She settled back in the chair. "'Our dearest daughter, we are so very sorry. It was our hope that we could keep you safe from the harshness of our world, but it looks as if we were unable to protect you as we had hoped if you are reading this letter. The woman that we hope will raise you will do a good job of keeping you in a fashion that we could not...safe and without harm.'"

"They were very nice people, despite being a little shy. But it was later that I figured out why they were keeping their distance." Margarita sat down as she continued. "A group of people came to the house a few days after you were brought to me. They asked if I had seen the couple next door and what had happened to them. I told them that I didn't know them well, but knew there had been a fire. They asked me about the child that was rumored to have been born to them. I had already decided that if anyone asked, I would never mention you weren't mine. So I told them that while I knew that the woman was with child, I had no idea if she'd given birth before that night."

Nodding, Vicki continued with the letter. "'We are life faeries. What that means for you is that you are a child of the earth. You can and will someday control it and the elements that come from it. Once you are able to say the words written here, you will become what you need to be. All knowledge of your life and your future will be yours for the taking.

"'We feel great sorrow that we cannot see you grow up into a fully-blossomed faerie. But it is our hope that you will not be a victim of the same trials as we have gone through to bring you into this world. We loved you, no matter the little time that we had with you. Go on with your life, love everything and everyone, and forgive us for leaving you to a stranger.'"

She put the letter down on her lap and stared around the room. Remy felt sorry for her. She'd had no idea that any of this, all of this, had happened without her knowledge.

"The malefactors have entered your home now that there is no one there to stop them. I believe that they have also taken your brother. Since the night that you came here, there has been no sighting of him, nor has he made any appearances at the usual places that your mother told us—"

"She's not my mother." Vicki flushed and looked at Margarita before speaking again. "You should have told me. Long before now, someone should have told me. I'm not an imbecile. I could have done something to protect myself."

"I was afraid that your father or brother would try to get you to do something that you would be hurt from. Worse than they do to me. You know how they were with me being a telepath." Vicki looked away from her. "I only meant to protect you from them."

"And this? What do you have to say about all of this?" Vicki looked back at her mom, then at Remy. "I want to leave here. Now. I don't want to stay here with you people any longer."

"It's not safe for you out there alone. They'll come for you now that you have my scent. Vicki, be—"

She cut Davis off. "If you tell me to be reasonable, I will hurt you." She stood up then and started pacing back and forth. Remy supposed it was more of a march than a pace, and she was doing it as she spoke in low tones, more than likely having a conversation with herself. When she left the room, just turning at the last minute and heading out of the room, no one moved to follow her. Not even Davis.

"I'll go." Skylar stood up and went to the door when Davis finally stood up. "You should give me a minute. I think talking girl to girl will be what she needs more than you telling her that you love her."

"I do. Love her I mean. I never thought that I'd find a woman to like me, much less love me. I don't want her to leave, but if she does, so will I." Skylar looked at Remy, then back at Davis as he continued. "I'm not going to follow you, but if you're not back in an hour, I'm coming to find you."

"All right." Skylar went out the door then, and Remy looked around the room. Margarita was crying softly, and Weston had disappeared...more than likely to shift back. Davis was looking like someone had hurt him, and Remy supposed in a large way Vicki had. Remy then wondered if she'd read all of the letter, including the words that may or may not have been at the bottom. And he wondered if Vicki even realized that what she'd read had not even been in English. Remy sat back in his chair.

"I have to go with her if she leaves here." Remy had already figured that out, but only nodded at his friend. "I don't want her to go. It's not safe out there for us, much less her. And with her being pissed off, I'm not sure she wouldn't just go out and take one on just to burn off some anger at us all."

"Maybe Skylar can help her with this. She's really good at talking to people." He hoped so anyway. "She might not think it's so bad once they have a little girl talk."

"Yeah, I'm not sure I'd like to know what either of them consider girl talk. They might just be trying to figure out which of us to murder first." Remy started to laugh and realized that Davis was serious.

"I think we should simply wait to see what happens before we go about thinking those kinds of thoughts." Davis said he'd wait, but he didn't sound all that convinced. Remy was afraid for all of them. Not just for the girl but for what was going on outside of this compound. The malefactors were getting stronger all the time.

Chapter 4

Vicki walked out into the yard and looked around. There were so many people, faded and blue men and women, standing around the property that it looked like a barrier had been set up that only they could see. She turned when someone said her name. Vicki turned back to the crowd as she spoke to Skylar.

"If you've come out here to see about changing my mind, you can forget it. I'm leaving." Skylar only snorted. "I have every right to leave here. And I plan to use those rights in getting back to my home. I know that I don't have a lot of say in it, but I can't stay here, not with her."

"By her, I'm assuming you mean the woman who gave up a lot to keep you safe all these years. The house you're talking about isn't going to happen anyway. It's locked up. Someone put a chain on the doors this morning. I could take you there if you don't believe me, but the landlord is suing you and your mother for back rent. Apparently there hasn't been a payment made in several months." Vicki started to deny that was possible, but she remembered the bruising on her mom—no, she wasn't her mom, but her face had been bruised a lot in the last few months. "It's not her fault she was trying to protect you. You have to know what it cost her to lie to you all this time."

"I never said it was her fault. But she did it all the same." Vicki turned to eye Skylar. "Are you reading my mind? And if so, I want you to stop right fucking now."

"I can, and I wouldn't have to if you'd just talk to us. I'm sure you have a lot of questions that you'd like answered. I can answer a few, but not all of them. Your mother will have to do that." Vicki stared at a couple of men who were trying to push another man into the circle. "They can't cross over into this land. It's warded with magic."

"And you're okay with thinking that?" Vicki turned to look at Skylar when she didn't answer. "Do you have any idea how off the wall you all sound? How out of touch with reality you are? And me too, I guess. I'm standing here, aren't I, listening to you?"

"Are we? Off the wall? Do you see my face? My arms? What do you see?" She told her that she was inked up. "What would you say if I told you that no human can see them? If asked to tell you what they see, they'd say that I was a woman. And that they don't see the monsters out there until they're bitten."

Vicki stared at the circle of malefactors and wondered what it was they were. "What are they? I mean, I can see them, and I'm not saying I believe you that no one can see them but us, but I would like to know what they are. And why are they here."

Skylar looked out over the vast field too. Vicki could see that there were hundreds of them. What were they doing here?

"They're called malefactors by us. Soldiers by their makers. And the blue ones are called adherents. I'm not sure what they are now, but at one time recently, they were people. And until a few months ago, like you, I had no idea what they were or why I could see them. But as to why they're here; it's something about stones and selling them to the highest bidder. Hector — you've met him — he said that they were created, the original ones anyway, to help fight wars on his realm. They were mindless killing machines that didn't know the word quit. And the reason they were brought here was to help us with our own. Or so we were told." Vicki waited for Skylar to go on while watching her face for any sign of insanity. It had to be that, no one could believe in other planets or realms or whatever they were. "Once they were here, they became mindless killing machines as they'd been on their own planet, but it was worse. They killed the good people as well as the bad. And they were no longer satisfied with just killing, but they started to turn them as well. Into what you see there. It wasn't until recently that we found out that they weren't sent here to help us, but to kill us all. All humans for a stone."

"A stone." Skylar nodded and bent and picked up one. "That is a worthless piece of agate. You can't expect me to believe that they came here for that."

"Watch." As she held it tightly in her hands, Vicki heard the monsters start to scream. As the stone turned to crumbles in Skylar's hand, the sound from the malefactors grew louder and louder. Then as she dropped the broken, almost completely dust stone, the people surrounding them began to try harder to get to them, killing several of their own in the process. But they never got any more than a foot over this invisible line at any time, and then it was only to die. From the sounds of it, it was a horrific and painful death too. "They're unable to come on to the property, as I've said. It keeps us safe. The house and all the people who live here are only able to enter because they are not associated with those things or the people who created them. And you have magic in you or you'd not know any of this."

"I don't have magic in me." She stared at the people, not wanting to believe a word Skylar was saying. "There's been a mistake. I don't want to be here. I don't want to be a faerie."

"I think it's too late for that, don't you?" Vicki nodded. "Davis is like us. Less than us, but like us. He has fangs, marks on him that he can and has pulled from his body to use as weapons. The sword at his back has saved many humans many times. I have wings, which you have seen on several occasions. Flown with me, as a matter of fact, twice now. To say that you don't believe us when we tell you we are magical is like saying that you don't believe your own eyes. And you do believe them, don't you, Vicki?"

"Why wasn't I told what I was long ago?" Skylar only shrugged. Vicki turned to the house when a door opened. Davis stood there on the patio watching them. "He said that I'm his mate. He's bitten me on several occasions. I've even…I've even bitten him. Does that make me a vampire?"

"It makes you his mate. Look at me, Vicki." Reluctantly, she looked at Skylar. "Do you think that I was born this way? That I came to this world looking like this, with wings and tats? I was just like you. A woman who had no past that was much of anything. No future at all because of something that was done to me without my knowledge. I am now a killing machine that works more hours than I should to try and keep the humans—as many as we can anyway—keep them from becoming what those things are."

Davis started toward them, and she felt her heart rate pick up. The man was gorgeous, big, and safe. Safe. It was a word she'd never used for another person in her life before. As he got closer, she glanced at Skylar when she stepped away and made her way back to the house. Vicki suddenly wanted everyone gone. Except for Davis.

An alarm went off somewhere within the house. She turned when he did, reaching for a weapon that she'd never carried before. Davis was tense, looking around as if he expected something to come at them at any moment. Then she saw it, high in the sky above them. Vicki was suddenly very glad for the magic that was surrounding them.

~~~

Davis pushed Vicki behind him when Benton landed a few feet from the border of their property. His monster was as big as he remembered him to be, but there was something very different about him. It took Davis a few seconds to figure out what it was. He was blue.

"What have we here? Fresh meat? Come here, little morsel, let me have a taste of you." Davis heard the others come out of the house but never took his eyes off Benton. He didn't think he could cross the line, but with him, who knew? "Come to me, girl. I'd like to add you to my harem."

"Well, well, if it's not Benton." The monster roared at Remy and made the big man smile. "Have you been away licking your wounds? Have you healed yourself enough that you wish another try at me? Come on now, come and get me."

"You think you're so funny, don't you, Rembrandt the Warrior?" Davis saw Remy stiffen, but he said nothing.

"Have you figured it out yet? Do you know where it is we know each other from?"

He was taunting Remy, and so far as he could see, Remy wasn't taking the bait. Instead he stared at the beast like he had all the time in the world to deal with him. The wings of Benton spread out, and he killed several of his men by beheading them with the sharp edges of his wings. Their bodies fell to the ground, their heads lolling around on the ground, blood spraying all over the big monster.

"Yes." Remy was very good at waiting. Davis had noticed that from the very beginning of their relationship. And his waiting this time obviously had the desired effect. Benton was pissed at him.

"I killed them, you know. All of them. I killed your entire family and had relations with your wife before I let the others have her. The house was burned to the ground on my orders. Your wife, the precious little woman, was raped by my say. Did you know that burning that barn of yours was the best thing I've witnessed in all my life? Watching those animals burn and scream for someone to save them? Your wife did much the same." Remy didn't move. He didn't even look as if he cared about what the big monster spewed at him. But as he continued, Davis noticed something happening to the monster. He was getting bigger. And meaner. "I had my way with her first, cutting the child from her as she lay there screaming for you to save her."

"She was dead long before you touched her. Took her own life rather than let any of you harm her. My children were not harmed by you either. They were hidden well below the house before you entered my home." The monster screamed as his wings spread out and waved great billows of air at them. "As for your order? I think not. You might believe that you did what you did, but those men you hired were not working for you but for another. They only took your coin when you offered it to them. My family died because I did not wish to fight for the wrong side."

"You lie." The spittle that spewed across the field burned in the dirt, bubbling up like acid. "You did not know me. You knew not that I was once your friend."

"You were never my friend, Augustus. But only a man that I felt sorry for when he had no one else."

He flew at them then, the big monster. Davis drew his sword but got no further than that. When Vicki stepped in front of him and raised her hands up, Benton flew back, his body on fire as something white and powerful spread from her fingers and toward him.

Vicki took a step toward the fallen beast, then another as power seemed to come from all around her. The ground shook, the trees bowed over, and the grass seemed to reach up for her. As she stood at the edge of the property, her fingers still burning into Benton's skin, he screamed, his voice echoing around the large area as if they were in a canyon and it bounced from there. As he took to the skies, his flesh still hot with the magic and burning debris dropping off him as his wings smoked behind him, Davis could see that he was sorely hurt. He might not even recover from it.

Davis looked at Vicki. Her hair was standing on end, swaying in the blowing air around her. Her body was a foot or more off the ground. The grasses that had reached for her just moments ago held her to them in a coil of their leaves. Davis thought perhaps they held her not to keep her from harm, but to keep her from going after the great monster that she'd hurt.

"Enough." Remy stepped in front of Vicki and pulled her hands down. "He's gone. Please, that's enough."

When he let her go, her hands dropped to her side, but she said nothing as she stared at Remy. Davis walked up behind her, his sword still in his hand, and put his free hand around her waist to pull her to his body. Remy still stared at her, saying nothing but holding her eyes with his own. When he finally turned away, his body shielding her seemingly, Vicki dropped. Had he not been there to catch her, scoop her up into his arms, Davis was sure she would have been hurt.

"Take her to your room. She'll need to rest for several hours, if not days." Davis started to ask Skylar how she knew that, but she spoke first. "This is the first time she's used these powers of hers, and I'm sure she's drained. We'll have the cook make her juices, lots of them. She's going to need them when she wakes."

"Will she be all right?" She shrugged, and he had an idea from her smile that she was going to be all right physically, but mentally she was going to be pissed off. "I'll call you if I need you."

"You won't." Skylar turned to Remy before speaking to them both. "We're going to have to explain what happened here today. Questions are going to need to be answered. Much of them from us. But whatever she did, it was powerful and dangerous. Hopefully she'll have more control over it than we did when we first began this."

Davis started for the house. Vicki was limp in his arms, but she was breathing and her heart was doing well. He was amazed that she'd done what she had. He had no clue what it was she'd done, but she'd done it. Simply stepping up to help them when she could have been hurt or even killed. As soon as he entered the house, he looked at Margarita.

"I won't hurt her." She nodded and smiled at him. "I won't. She's my life, my love. I didn't think I'd ever say those words, but there you have it."

"She's all I ever wanted in a daughter and then some. She could have gone off and left me alone to deal with her half-brother, but she never did. Even with him being mean to us all the time, she never left me." Davis pulled Vicki closer to his body. "Please care for her in ways that I could never do."

"I will." She nodded and opened the door to the lower levels for him. As he moved down the stairs toward his room, he looked down at her face. He was still amazed as her beauty. Her eyes opened just as he entered his room.

"You're going to be fine." Nodding, she just stared at him. Then she bowed up in his arms and screamed. It was all he could do to hold onto her without dropping her. But even as he laid her down on his bed, he could see the markings on her body begin to appear. She slipped away just as the marks started.

It took only seconds, about as long as his had taken to come to his body. But he knew that the pain was going to be lingering. Not as intense as it was at first, but still painful. The marks were the same, but as he watched hers form, blood dripping off her body in rivers, he knew that soon he'd be in just as much pain, for she was being marked with some that he did not have.

When they were both marked, Davis picked her up and took her to the bathroom. He wanted her cleaned of the drying blood before she woke again. He was pressing her against the tile just outside the shower when she woke again. He grinned at her when she asked him what he thought he was doing.

"I'm trying to take all your clothing off. You know, this isn't as easy as I thought it would be. They make it look so easy in the movies, don't they?" She smacked his hands away and pulled her blouse up over her head. He felt his cock thicken with need at the sight of her bare body. "I was going to wash you up from the blood."

"I'm marked." He nodded and dropped to his knees in front of her, pulling off her shoes one at a time. He knew that she was overwhelmed when she said nothing to him about what he was doing. And when he kissed her inner thigh, she started talking again. "I didn't know that I could do that to that…whatever it was that I just did. But I could feel that he was going to hurt you all. His flame would have breached the barrier and he would have hurt you all."

"That power that came from you…I think the earth gave you a bit of itself too. Do you know how you did that?" She shook her head, and he leaned into her belly and kissed the bare warm flesh. "Doesn't matter. You did very well on your first time out."

"I was terrified. But I knew…somehow I knew that if I didn't do something then, all of us would have been dead. What if I had hit one of you guys with that…that was crazy power, wasn't it?" He nodded and kissed her hip as he pulled her pants down a little further. "I've never felt that way before either. Wanting to kill someone." She let out a long breath when he swirled his tongue in her navel. "You're making me crazy. I'm not going to sleep with you."

"That's good. I don't want to sleep with you either." He pulled her pants down to her knees and buried his mouth over her heat, tasting as much as he could before lifting his head and looking up at her. "I want to make love to you all night, eat you until I'm full, then fuck you again. And if you want, you can do anything you'd like to me. I'll be your willing slave."

"Davis." He leaned into her again, pulling the small lace to the side as he slid his tongue between her nether lips. She was wet, hot, and so wet for him. Davis drank from her as she canted her hips to his mouth. "Please. We can't have sex standing up. It's not right."

He suckled her clit into his mouth and bit down. Not hard enough to draw blood, but enough to have her crying out his name. As he slid his fingers into her sheath, sucking and lapping at her the entire time, she spread her legs for him, and he lifted her up by her ass to bring her pussy tighter to his mouth. Davis watched her face as he ate her.

It wasn't enough for him, but she was enjoying herself over and over as he continued to taste her. When she begged for him to stop, crying that she'd had enough, Davis lay her on the floor and continued to feast on her. When her legs wrapped around his head, Davis willed his clothing gone and fisted his cock.

"Fuck me." He let go of her clit, sucking the hard nubbin into his mouth again before lifting his body from hers. As he made his way up her, nipping and biting her as he went, Davis marked her with his teeth, leaving small scars in his wake until he got to her breasts.

"I'm going to feed from you here." She nodded and pulled his head to her right breast. As soon as his fangs sank into her Vicki came, screaming out his name even as he entered her.

Her tight sheath fit him like a glove. Lifting his body up, giving himself plenty of room, he pounded her hard, watching her face as she tightened once again around his cock. Davis moved to her throat, felt her pounding pulse with his tongue, and bit deeply into her, drinking from her as her body came for him again.

Her fingers tightened in his hair and she lifted him up. When he saw her mouth, her sharp fangs lengthened and stretched out beyond her lip, Davis felt his cock fill and his balls tighten around his body. Leaning to her, his cock buried as deep as he could get it, he offered her his throat and exploded, came apart inside of her when she bit him.

He brought her again by sliding his hand under her ass and pulling her to him. He emptied hard and fast, his cock filling again as she wrapped her legs around him. When she screamed out his name, still at his throat, Davis bit into her shoulder, his body releasing once again. He fell atop her then, his entire being exhausted and sated. Davis thought about moving off her, taking her to his body, but there was nothing left for him to move, much less move her too.

He lay there on top of her, not thinking about anything but how good he felt...how much he was in love with her. Ignoring what had happened in the yard and how she'd evolved with him, Davis lifted his head just enough to look into her eyes and saw the change in them. They were no longer blue, but now were every shade he could think of.

"You should see you how I see you." Vicki nodded once and closed her eyes. "No. I want to watch them. You have no idea how gorgeous they are right now. How simply beautiful you are to me with all the magic within you."

"Yours too. They're like incandescent lights all brightly colored for fall and Christmas at once. Your skin is glowing too; even your hair looks like its sparking from the tips." Her fingers ran down his cheek to his neck. "I bit you. Fed from you."

"You did." When her eyes lifted to his, he could see tears there and wondered what was wrong.

"I don't want to be this thing." He nodded and laid his head on her breast. Her hands danced along his back, relaxing him in ways that sex usually did. "What was that that came from me, Davis? Is that what I am? A powerhouse of energy?"

"That's as good an answer as I can come up with." He looked at her again. "You saved us. All of us. We might have been burned to death without you there."

"I didn't have a clue what I was doing. But this...like need came up from my arms and I had to use it." He smiled at her. "What?"

"We're all doing that. None of us have a clue what we are, what we're doing. It's like we're fumbling around in the dark without a flashlight. Just by accident I discovered I could do this." He put up his hand and wiggled his fingers. Light shot from them in a rainbow of colors. "I don't have the slightest clue what I'd use it for, but I can do it. And I can dress and undress myself with just a thought. Remy actually told me about that one. Oh, and since I met you and we've been...feeding, I have wings. I didn't have those before you."

Vicki put up her fingers and did the same thing he'd done. He told her to think of lights, and suddenly there were brilliant lights dancing from the tips of hers as well. She sat up then, almost knocking him across the room in her haste. As she rolled off the floor and stood up, he watched her change from one outfit to another. It was the sexiest thing he'd ever witnessed.

A dress, a pair of pants...then there was a gown, a coat. She went from one thing, one mode of dress, to the next in dizzying speed. And all of them fit her like they'd been tailored for her. When she turned to him, grinning, he had to smile.

"This is so much better than anything I've ever done before. I could be...." Her dress was suddenly gone, and she was dressed in a pair of black leather pants, black tee, and boots. "I can be as sloppy or as dressy as I want with just a thought. This is so way cool."

"Which is this? Because right now all I can think of is how fucking incredibly sexy you look dressed all in black. And damn, woman, you wear it well." The clothing was gone, and she stood before him in a pair of the smallest panties he'd ever seen and the sexiest bra that barely covered her nipples. "Fuck me."

"Okay." She was on him before he could reach for her. Vicki laid him back on the floor and sat over his cock. "I could really get used to this too. Sex whenever I want it. Who knew that it could be so amazingly wonderful?"

Davis started to tell her he did, but she was riding him, her pussy tightly wrapped around his cock while she rode him hard. Reaching up, he cupped her breasts and pulled hard on her nipples as she hummed out her pleasure. Yeah, Davis thought, he could get used to this as well.

Chapter 5

The hoard was moving toward one of the larger apartment buildings. Davis was right behind them but on foot. He still wasn't great with the wings yet. He figured that knocking over two of the big bushes in the yard and nearly decapitating Remy meant that he needed more practice. Of course the big man had laughed, but still.... Davis looked over at Vicki as they were set to round the corner to the building.

"Just cut off their heads. And according to Remy, the turquoise on the blade will make it kill quicker if you just touch it to their skin." She nodded but looked nervous. "If you want to go back, now is the time. No one expects you to do this your first time out."

"One of those pricks might have hurt someone I know." He nodded. They more than likely had. There was still no word from her brother, but even in his meanness, he knew that she was worried about him. "I can do this. I can really do this."

There was no doubt that she could physically do this. But he worried about her mentally. He had killed before.

Not a lot, but he'd been a cop for a lot of years before coming to help Remy. She'd been a nurse…a damned fine one too he'd bet. There was a great difference in what she was about to do.

They moved around the corner, and before he could move toward them there was a shrill whistle right next to him. He looked at Vicki just as she pulled her fingers from her lips. He was so impressed that that sound had come from her he nearly missed what she said next.

"You fuckers have been here long enough. It's time you either change your ways or we're going to fuck you up." She winked at him before continuing. "Of course, we're going to kill you anyway, but we'd like to take this opportunity to give you the chance to repent."

They came at them…nearly fifty, he'd say, but they were coming. As he lifted his sword, he looked at Vicki once more to make sure she was going to be all right, just as she sliced through the first two that came close. Davis smiled. She was going to be just fine.

They worked for nearly an hour. His arm was sore, his body covered in blood. He'd lost sight of Vicki twice as they worked, but she appeared just before he was ready to go look for her. She sat next to him now in the mire and looked as bad as he did. The dead were all around them, their faded bodies nothing more than fodder now. Before he got too comfortable, he got up to search for the stones. They were collecting them so that no one else, Benton or the other two, could reuse them. Vicki started helping him when he showed her what to look for.

"I knew two of them. The dead, I mean." He nodded. He'd noticed the lab coats as well and wondered if she might. "One was a prominent surgeon. Another was a nurse like me. They're dead now. Not because of me but just because. Do we know why?"

"Just that they want to take this planet from us. Something about these stones and selling them to another planet." She nodded and two more of the soldiers walked in front of them. Before he could stand and take them out, she put up her hand and they were incinerated. "Christ, how did you do that?"

"I have no idea. I was going to stretch out my arm before I got up to help you kill them. And there it was." She put her hands under her butt as if she were afraid of what she could do too. "This shit is too cool, and scary as hell too."

"Yeah. I agree." As they sat there after they'd found all the stones they could, he thought about all the things that Remy and Skylar could do and wondered if, as the other men came to them, they'd have the same discoveries. He decided that he'd make a list of abilities and how to do each of them. Maybe it would keep one or more of them from taking off a friendly's head.

"I'm going to work with Weston. I want to help you as well, but I think I'd like to work in the clinic too. I was a good nurse. My mom...my mom is going to help him as well. She was very close to becoming a doctor when my dad died. Maybe she can help him out a little like that as well." Davis was glad that she'd come to terms with her mom. He knew that they'd talked a long time last night and again this morning. Things were still a little tense, but at least she was calling her Mom. "These other men, the ones that are coming to help us, do you know who they might be? And what they'll be able to do when they get here?"

"No. We know nothing about them. We have a list of six names. Remy has it. Remy and I were each one of the names on it, so there are at least four more that we don't know. Remy thinks they're going to come to us a few at a time. Hector was helping with that, but he's sort of out of the loop now. I think...the men he worked with want him dead now. He betrayed them to help us."

"Rueben said that his mom was killed by some bad men. I just assumed it was some of the malefactors." Davis shook his head. "These other guys? What do we know about them? I mean, we have some idea what we're up against, right?"

"It was some of the people who created these things. Ward is one of them, and Dolin is the other. I don't think they have last names. At least Hector doesn't have one, so I'm assuming they won't either. And his son nearly died too when the mom did. The blood of the dead, that's what they were feeding the two of them before Rueben got here. I guess Mrs. Hector couldn't take it as well as her boy." Two more malefactors came around the corner toward them. Before Vicki could raise her hand up, he raised his. A blast of energy came out of his hand and blew both of them apart. "I suppose we could just sit here and take them out as they come around."

"Not very sporting of us, is it? Not that I really care. These things have had enough sport with us to last me a lifetime." He sat there smiling. Who knew that killing someone, or in this case something, could be so much fun? "Davis, what happens to us?"

"Us?" She nodded. "I don't...you and I are mates, I guess. I'm not really sure what that means, but I'm happy with the term. I love you. I think you're going to live forever, like me, and I'm thrilled to death to know that you're going to be by my side during our life. Are you?"

"Yes. But that's not what I mean." She looked frustrated. "When this is done...do we go back to our old selves? I mean, I'm a faerie and you're a...what are you, anyway?"

"Remy said we're warriors. Vampires too, I suppose, but not like in the books you read. I can take the sunlight, eat when I want. I don't need to go to the earth, as women's books call it. I like it, warrior. Sounds like I'm going to be big and bad-assed. You are too." He picked her up and put her on his lap. "You can be my warrior, and I'll be yours. And if you want to be a nurse, that's fine with me too. So long as at the end of the day, we're together."

"You're such a dork." He kissed her nose and let her go when she started to stand. As she pulled him up, nearly slinging him across the street, he smiled down at her.

"I love you." She grinned. "You can say it too. I won't make fun of you. Okay, I might a little, but not very much."

"I...I like you a great deal. You're a good lay. But love you? I'm not sure yet. I need time." He nodded. Davis could wait for her. They had a long time to get to know each other and be together. "You're really okay with that?"

"For now." They were heading to the car when she stiffened beside him. He nearly asked her what it was, but she was staring at a man across the street, and from the stance she was taking, he'd bet anything it was her brother. He leaned into her ear to whisper to her. "Concentrate on him and you can hear him if you want."

She shook her head, but he knew she was hearing him despite the fact that she might not want to. One of the perks they'd gotten, he supposed, was excellent hearing. He focused all his hearing on the man too. It was time the bastard got some payback.

"Yeah, she can do just about anything. And if you get busted up, she's a nurse too." Davis wondered if it was his mom or sister he was talking about until he continued, "And so fine too. Fuckable fine. My sister is gonna make you millions. All I want from you is some cash up front to buy her out."

"Buy her out of what?" That's what Davis wanted to know, but waited. "You say she has some sort of mind thing going on, but you're really vague. You tell me she's fuckable; not even sure what that means, but you've no picture. You're selling goods that you have no proof of. For all I know, you could be a cop."

Her brother nodded and reached into his coat pocket. The gun was out, and he fired at the man coming up the street behind the man he'd been talking to. "I'm not a cop. I'm a fucking guy that's going to make you a millionaire. But if you ain't buying, I'll just find me someone else."

As he started to walk away, Davis could see the smile when the man said his name. Randall knew when he had a mark as well as Davis did. As they watched, the two of them set up a deal. Randall had one week to produce something about his sister or the deal was off.

"And that money I'm spotting you will be returned to me if you fuck me over. With interest." Randall kissed the cash and nodded. "You're one fucking bastard, aren't you?"

"Yes I am. I am at that." He walked away, stuffing the gun and the money in his pocket. Another man peeled away from the wall down the street just as Randall passed him. Davis knew a tail when he saw one. Who the man worked for was unknown for now. After Randall moved by the alley he and Vicki were in, they made their way to the car. He wasn't worried about the guy knowing Vicki. He'd already said he had no picture. As soon as they were in the car and he was moving down the road to the compound, Vicki started crying.

"What a prick. I mean, I knew he was horrible, but he just sold me. For what? To be that guy's...." She looked at him. "He said I could do things with my mind. That means...how did Randall know? I didn't even know. And busted up? Does he really expect me to just fix this bastard up when he's planning to use me for...whatever he wants?"

"I have no idea, but I'm sure your mom knows how he found out. And as for him using you, that's not going to happen either. First of all, you're not the same person you were when he knew you back then, and I'm pretty sure if given the chance, I could take him too." She nodded, but he could tell she was far from all right. As she worked out her own demons, he tried to think what he'd do if he were still a cop. Tagging the guy was a good way to go, but it would be hard for him to get close enough to do that. He could send someone after him to keep an eye on him, but who? Davis was still working and planning as they drove up on the compound. But the sight that was there nearly had him forget the entire thing. It was the funniest sight he'd ever seen.

~~~

"I can do this." Remy nodded but didn't touch Skylar. She was pissed off enough without him trying to show her again. The sword was entirely too big for her, but she'd insisted that she wanted to learn how to use it. Not to mention that she was just too fucking cute not to watch.

She'd decided that the blade that she had wasn't doing what she wanted it to. He had no idea what she wanted it to do more than cut the heads off malefactors, but she wanted him to show her. So they'd ended up outside with an audience. Seven of them.

At first it had only been Ann and Margarita. They'd been working in the little garden just behind the building when they'd first come out, and had pulled up chairs since. Then a few minutes later, Catherine and the baby came out. The kid was just starting to look at things, but Remy didn't count him in the people watching her. Jarvis had come out with Weston, and then Davis and Vicki had shown up, all of them in chairs and each of them having a good time. So was Remy, if he was truthful about it. Of course, he was quiet about it, but he was having fun. When Skylar tipped over again, he had to turn his back to her so she'd not remove his head.

"Maybe if you just shortened your foot stance." Skylar looked over at Davis and asked him what he meant. Standing, he showed her how to place her feet. "That's it. Now instead of swinging with your hands, use your body."

Vicki said she wanted to learn as well, and he and Davis were standing behind their mates showing them when a man walked out of the malefactors and toward them. All of them paused and Catherine picked up the baby and went to the house. Davis was holding Vicki's hands down and Remy wondered about that, then remembered the other day with Benton. Yeah, he thought, good idea until they knew if he was friend or foe. When the man stopped and put out his hand to shake, Remy stepped in front of the other three. The man seemed to understand and only nodded at him.

"Leonard Earl. Everyone calls me Leo. I think you were expecting me." The man neither looked happy to be there nor thrilled about meeting them. Remy put out his hand, but didn't introduce the others to him just yet. "I've come a long way, killing those things as I went. I've been...it's been a long two weeks, and I'm not even sure what the fuck I'm doing. Do you have a fucking clue why I'm here?"

"Nope."

Leo nodded and looked at the building. "A man in black, all black, came to me about five months ago. Said I was to come here and help you with the monsters. I've tried my best to ignore the need to come here. But things…there have been some changes in me that I can't explain. I thought if you told me what was going on, I could, I don't know, move on anyway. I don't have any desire to help you no matter what he did for me."

"I don't think it works that way." Leo looked at Davis when he spoke. "What's your power? I'm not sure what you'd call it, but ability then. If you've survived this long without help, then you must be able to do something that has kept you from harm."

"If you mean bite and feed from someone, that's something I never did before. But since…lately I can do all kinds of weird shit. Like this." He moved his hand over his shoulder and came out with a long sword. It was thin and the handle—the pummel—was covered in a thick dark leather. There were turquoise stones all down the blade, so tiny it was almost as if the thing were made of them. "I can use it too. Like I've had lessons. And this sucker is a part of me. I mean, literally a part of me."

"Great. Someone else to show us how to use the weapons we have." He was shaking his head at Skylar even as she handed him her sword. "They say it's too big for me. How would you change it?" Remy watched as Skylar just moved in, trying to make the man help her even when it looked as if he didn't want to be there.

"Look, lady. I can see you need help and all, but I'm not going to be doing the training. I just wanted to come here and move on. This guy, he said you'd know what I was here for." Remy smiled as he heard Rueben coming out of the house. And he was sure that Hector was right behind him. "I'm not cut out to be a team player. I'm more of a lone wolf that—"

"Are you?" The question startled him, Remy could tell, but Reuben didn't stop asking. "Are you a wolf? Weston is, and so is Jarvis. And when Catherine is well enough, she's gonna be one too. I can't be one. I'm too small."

"Am I a what?" Leo looked at Remy, then Reuben again. "There are no such things as men who can change into wolves, kid. Whoever told you that was lying to you. I don't know where you got that idea, but we're all just—"

"I'm a faerie. This woman is Skylar...I'm not sure what she is, but she's awesome. Weston there is a doctor who also happens to be a wolf." Leo kept up with her, shaking hands that were offered when Vicki made the rounds of introductions to the rest of the people that had gathered. "And you are a warrior. That's what we all are when it comes down to it. You might not like it. Hell, none of us do, but that's what you are. So either work with us or go out there with the malefactors, let one of them turn you, and someday real soon, one of us will kill you. I'm hoping right now that it'll be me. I really hate whiny people."

Leo looked at Remy, then back at Vicki. "You always this welcoming? Or is there a reason you're being particular nasty to me? I've had a really shitty few months, and the only reason I'm here is because the need to be here has been keeping me up at night. I'm hoping that now that I'm here I'm over it and can get on with my life. Even as fucked up as it is."

"I'm not normally nasty to anyone unless you piss me off. Which, in the event you didn't get it, you have. I was in a really good mood until you came in and shit on my fun." She lifted her hand and blasted through about a dozen malefactors before continuing. "To think, if Davis hadn't stopped me, that could have been you."

She turned and walked away. Remy stared at her for several seconds before he threw back his head and laughed. Christ, she was as bad as Skylar. Not that he'd point that out to either woman. It wasn't that he'd thought they'd be mad, no. He was afraid they'd start double-teaming them and kill them all. He put out his hand to Leo.

"Welcome to our house of madness. I'm sure that there's a room for you inside. Talk to Ann about any food you might require. Also, have Catherine show you around. But don't touch her. Her mate is very possessive. And a wolf too."

Leo nodded but didn't move. He did, however, take his hand, and Remy felt a connection. It was sharp and quick, and he knew that something profound had been touched off as soon as Leo let him go. The man dropped to the ground, crying out in pain.

It was all Remy could do not to flip the man over and see where he'd been hurt. But he knew what was happening. The man was being marked. Just like with all of them, his power would come to him stronger now, and whatever he could do now, when his mate came, it would be even stronger.

"Mother fuck." He looked up at him, and Remy knelt down to his level. "What the fuck did you do to me?"

"I think I might have just claimed you into our band. Sort of like matching jackets, but we have tats." Remy waited until the man sat on his ass and looked up at him before he spoke again. "What are you? I'm assuming you're human, but what were you before this?"

"School teacher. Fifth grade." He looked around while he sat there. "I was also dying. I had just been diagnosed with leukemia about a month before. It was...I only had six weeks to live. Then while I was in the hospital, this guy comes along and tells me he has plans for me. And that I was to come here. I don't suppose you know why me?"

"That would have been Hector, I think. That's him over there with the little boy." The man looked at him, then lunged at Hector. He backed away but said nothing as he shielded his son from harm. Remy nodded. "I'm assuming this is the man who touched you."

Hector walked toward them then. Not close enough to be touched should Leo try again, but he'd left Rueben in the care of the others while he stood there. Leo looked up at him as he sat there. Remy knew the man was still in a great deal of pain.

"Yes. You motherfucker, why me?" Hector looked at Remy, then at Leo before he sat down too. Hector looked around before he spoke, but Leo cut him off when he opened his mouth. "And how the hell did you make me tatted with this blade? And this shit, what the hell is this?"

"You are marked as a warrior, as you've been told. But I will admit to you that I have no idea of the rest. Like the people of this household, there have been changes to you as well as them that I did not do. In fact, I had no idea that any of this—other than you were all to come here—was going to happen." Hector nodded to Remy as he continued. "I only changed this man. At first I gave him life, long life, and the ability to see the monsters I needed him to kill. The rest—everything that each of them can do, including you— are developments that they have gotten on their own. The tats on your back, the ones I'm assuming you have on your legs, I had nothing to do with those either. I have surmised that they are part of the magic that will keep you and those around you safe. What is your super power? You have one; have you found it yet?"

"Superpower? You mean more than I have right now with this sword?" Hector nodded at Leo, and he started cursing again. "I have no idea. I was a man who had nothing to live for. No hope of recovering from this illness that took everything from me. The next thing I know the doctors are scratching their heads and wondering what the hell happened. And so was I. You did this to me."

"I did." Hector looked up at Remy, then at Leo. "I did save you. I have to...the person that is a warrior, like the malefactors that are out there, must be close to death before I can convert them. All of you, all the men who are coming here to work together, have been so close to death. It was the only way to save you so that you could work with Remy and the others. Had I not, you'd be dead now."

"I didn't want to be saved." Hector stood up and left Leo sitting in the grass with Remy. He looked at Remy before he spoke again. "I was dying. Ready. My mother was gone. I lost my house when I got sick. Everything that meant something to me was gone because of this illness that I'd never counted on. I didn't even have a dime to bury me with. But I was ready. My life up until that man came to me was over, and now this."

"But you're here now. And we need you." Leo was still sitting there when Remy went into the house. And an hour later, Leo was still out there. But now he was sitting next to Vicki. Remy could see that neither of them were speaking, but they seemed to be connecting. He wondered what was going to happen.

"She saw her brother today." Remy looked at Davis when he spoke behind him. "He was selling her. Or I guess he actually sold her. To some guy. He made promises to him about her being a good fuck as well as able to do things with her mind. I think he hurt her badly. I can feel her sorrow, but I'm not sure if it's because we're going to kill him or that he'd done this to her."

"Both, I would imagine." Remy watched Vicki with Leo. "He's not going to be much help if he doesn't get the chip off his shoulder. Right now he's just trying to adjust to things. I understand that, but he's not of much use to us just sitting on his ass. What can we do to fix this?"

"She'll bring him around. I don't know why, but I think he might need someone like her to kick him in the ass a little." Davis moved away then, and Remy stood there watching. He had no idea what to think of either of the men that now worked with him. But one thing was for sure, it was going to be an adventure.

Remy stood there until Leo stood up. He offered his hand to Vicki, who didn't take it right away. There were words spoken—he was sure that they were caustic coming from the woman—but Leo only nodded and then laughed. Remy thought that things might be a little better now. Not perfect—nothing so far had been—but it might go a little easier on the man. And in turn them as well. But as soon as they walked through the door together, he thought maybe he'd been a little premature. They were still arguing at the top of their lungs as they went to the lower levels. Ann tisked at him when he paused on the stairs. Both of them could hear what was being said below them.

"He'll need to clean up his mouth if he hangs around the baby much. If his first words are 'fucking asshole,' I'm going to give Leo salt peter in his meals for the rest of his life." Remy laughed but said nothing. "You mark my words. First time Carter says one of those words and he's just a little man, I'm going to hurt that man."

"I'm sure once he hangs around a while, he'll change his tune." Remy hoped so anyway. The man simply projected anger. "Maybe he can take you out and show you how to use his sword."

She flushed, and as Remy walked away, he realized how dirty that had sounded. He nearly went back to tell Ann that's not what he meant, but figured it would be worse. Instead, he went to find Skylar. Maybe she'd let him show her how he used his sword.

Chapter 6

Vicki was in the gym when she heard her mom. There had been several opportunities to talk to her over the last several days, but she'd not wanted to get into an argument with her. And Vicki was sure there would be one. Instead, she'd been avoiding her. But they had to talk.

"I'm sorry. I didn't know anyone was in here. I'll come back later." Vicki almost let her mom go but called her back. "I just wanted to use the hot tub. I can do that later."

"I saw Randall." That had her turning back. "He never saw me or he might not be up and around, but he sold me to some guy. I don't know for how much, but it looked like a nice bundle of cash. How did he know what I am?"

Her mom came into the room and sat near one of the many benches. "He figured it out. Not what you are, but that you weren't my daughter. He came to me a few months ago, right after you moved in with me, and asked me what you were, and who you were."

"And what did you tell him?" She sat there looking so afraid that Vicki went to sit next to her on the bench. "I'm not upset anymore. I know how he is. Did he hurt you, Mom? Did he knock you around to make you tell him?"

"I tried to fight him, but he's so much stronger than I am. I could tell...he'd been drinking or high when he got into the house. I'd been bringing in the groceries the cabbie helped me put on the sidewalk. It was difficult to do with this chair, but I'd managed pretty well. I had just shut the door to the house when I realized he'd gotten in while I was going back for the last bags. He showed me the letter. I guess he'd been looking for money and found it." She rolled her chair to the large tub and started the jets. She didn't get in yet, but she did dangle her fingers in the water, stalling, Vicki thought. "He hit me a few times, knocked me into the wall and out of my chair. Then he sat on me and beat my head into the floor until I told him. I thought he was going to kill me. I must have said something then."

"How did he know what the letter said?" Vicki had found out just yesterday that the letter she'd read wasn't in English, but in a language that no one knew. Even with the help of Jarvis and Jake using the computer, they had found was nothing about the language. "Was he able to read it?"

"No. I didn't...no. He said he knew what it said. And like a fool I believed him. So I asked him if it was from your parents, about the night they'd brought you to me. He said it told how they weren't human. I had an idea that you weren't like us, but he said you weren't human. I guess...I sort of told him I knew what you were. And that...I told him you could read minds and manipulate them. I'm so sorry."

"He has no idea that I'm a faerie then?" Her mom shook her head as she continued to play in the water, not looking at her. Vicki could tell that she was crying. She wiped at the tears several times while she sat there. "So all he thinks is that I'm different, but not how much."

"I tried to tell him that you weren't very good at it yet. Even told him that without proper training you'd not be able to do much more than hurt someone. I had no idea. But he didn't believe me anyway. Not until a couple of days later, the day that you guys came to get me, did I really know how different you are." She smiled at her. "I saw you blast those monsters out there today. I'm very proud of you."

Vicki flushed. She wasn't very proud of herself. She'd been showing off and pissed. Vicki knew better than anyone that losing your temper could be bad for everyone. Watching her mom, she smiled.

"I heard that Weston said he could help you with your back. He said that surgery would make it so you could walk again." Her mom told her she was afraid. "We're all afraid of something and someone, Mom. But if he can help you to walk again, I'd very much like that. Maybe you could meet a really nice man that will treat you right this time."

"No thank you. Good heavens, girl. Who would I...?" Her mother looked at her with the most comical look on her face. "You should know better than anyone that one man in my life was enough. I don't need, nor do I ever want, another person who can have the privilege of knocking me around. And so you know, that nice young wolf is showing me how to fight back. He said that every woman should be able to. Even the ones in wheel chairs."

Vicki got up and kissed her mom on the cheek. "I think it's a great idea. And it's good for you. Just don't go turning into a wolf on me. I don't know if I could handle too much more change in my life right now."

"This young man, Davis, he's making you happy, isn't he?" Vicki nodded. "I'm glad for you both. I think he's in love with you."

"He said he is. But like you, I'm a little on the shy side when it comes to men and their fists. Once might have been enough for me as well." Her mother asked if she loved him. "I think so. I'm not...like you, I'm not ready for a person in my life like this. He's not like dad was. Nothing like Randall either, but it's a big change for me. All of this is a lot to take on right now."

"I understand." Her mother turned and pulled off her robe. She was sliding into the water when Vicki realized someone had put the tub in for her, and that it more than likely had healing powers. "I'm feeling better about a lot of things since we've been here. Not just with being safe, but with the magic that's here. It's a wonderful thing to see people using it for good and not for bad things, like your stepfather or Randall would have. Once this is all done, with these monsters and stuff, I'm going to find me a nice house out there and play in the dirt again. It was fun doing it today, and I didn't feel handicapped once."

Vicki left her mom a few minutes later. She was worried about her brother. Not as much as when she'd been living at home, but she still worried for her mom. But everyone here seemed to work together to keep everyone safe. Ann said that she was going to ask for panic buttons by the doors, just in the event that someone came to the door that shouldn't be there. Vicki thought maybe she'd talk to Skylar about it. But she was nervous about that too. Skylar was one scary bitch.

The kitchen was at the right at the top of the stairs. She walked in just as Leo and Ann were talking. She was still a little upset with the man, but she was willing to give him some slack. Not much, but a little. The knock at the door had her thinking about the button again, and she nearly fell backwards when Ann, who had opened the door, was shoved back. Leo was knocked out of his chair, and his head hit the floor hard. He didn't move as she tried to get to Ann, who was struggling with a large person.

The man, who had come into the room screaming at them, never stopped hitting and slapping anyone that had the misfortune to be too close, which was mostly Ann. He had her in a headlock when he realized that Vicki had the door blocked.

"You stay there or so help me, you'll be next. Get that girl. I want her home with me right fucking now." Vicki was willing to try and be reasonable, but the fear on Ann's poor battered face pissed her off. "Are you fucking deaf, girl? I said to get my daughter and that spawn of hers. I want them now."

"You're not welcome here. And if you don't leave right now, I'm going to kick your ass all the way across the yard." He hit Ann again, this time knocking her head against the cabinets. Vicki had had enough and hit him back.

The man was big, huge, and sloppy. His fists were hard, mean, and he had on a ring that bit deeply into her flesh. But Vicki was used to dealing with men who used their fists instead of their words to get what they wanted. He hit Ann again while Vicki tried to gain her footing to attack again.

"Where the fuck is she?" Ann was bleeding and tried to get away from the man, but he jerked her back by the hair and back handed her. As Ann went falling again, this time atop Leo's inert body, Vicki stood up and lunged herself at the stranger. He hit her twice before she got herself behind him. Then she jerked his neck hard to the right and heard the snap. Dropping him, she fell to her knees. Fuck, she'd just killed him.

~~~

Leo staggered down the stairs. His head was bleeding badly, and he thought perhaps his arm was broken. As soon as he got to the bottom of the staircase, he fell against the computer table in front of him. Three men, one of them he thought was Davis, came at him.

"The women." He felt himself being picked up and before he knew it, he was being taken back up the stairs. He had no clue why he was being carried up instead of put on a bed so he could just die. But when Remy, he could see now, sat him on a chair, he could see that Vicki had not moved since he'd left her.

"Vicki?" Leo stood up and blocked Davis from touching her. He'd done that already before going to get some help. He was pretty sure it was the reason his arm was killing him. She'd been really pissed when he'd tried to see if she was all right. "I need to see—"

"Don't touch her. She's a little spaced out right now and will fucking hurt you." Davis looked at her, then at him. "I tried to see if she was all right before coming to get you guys, and she tore into me like a bear. Just let her come back to us. Talk to her. That might work. But just don't touch her. She's not herself."

Davis nodded and went to sit across from her. Ann was being attended to, and when she sat up she burst into tears. Leo wasn't a whiny man, nor was he a big complainer before all this shit. But he thought about joining her. Christ, there wasn't a part of him that didn't hurt right now.

"Do you know what happened up here?"

Leo nodded and then shook his head. That sent a whole new kind of pain to his head, and he held it while he looked at Remy. The man was smiling at him. Not in a scary way, but like he was genuinely amused at him.

"I fucking hurt, all right?" Remy nodded and sat in the other chair. The fourth one was busted all to hell, so he watched the doc—Weston, he thought his name was—leaning against the counter while he stared at him. Ann was holding an ice pack to her face. "Vicki and I entered this room about the same time. Ann was already in here, and I thought about getting to know her. But someone knocked on the door. Not like he was asking permission to come in, but knocked it back on its hinges like he wanted the fucker busted in. He barged in, yelling about having someone brought to him, and grabbed Ann. I have no idea if he said their name, the people he wanted. But by the time I'd tried to stand up again to throw him out, he'd hit Ann and threw her into me. After that, I have no idea. I woke up to see Vicki leaning over the dead man and bleeding. When I touched her to see if she was okay, she went a little ape shit and nearly took my arm off. After checking on Ann, I went to find you guys."

"I think he was looking for Catherine." Vicki never moved from where she was, and she wasn't looking at them either as she spoke. "He knocked Ann down several times, and I tried to reason with him. I reasoned with him when I knew that there is no reasoning with men like him. I should have just thrown him out of the house and come for you guys. But I didn't."

"What happened, Vicki?" Remy's voice was low but firm. Vicki kept looking at the dead man, so he repeated his question.

"I hit him a couple of times. Told him to get out. But he was set on getting her. And every time he got close enough to Ann, he'd hit her again." Vicki finally looked up and right at Ann. "He's your ex-husband, the one that Catherine told me about?"

"He is." Ann looked down at him. "He was, I guess. You saved me. I can't tell you enough how happy I am that you were in here when you were. And you too, Mr. Leo. I think he…he would have killed me if not for you two. Because as surely as I'm sitting here, he wasn't going to get my girl."

"I didn't do that much but be a cushion for your fall. He might have killed you both for all the help I was." Ann shook her head and put her hand over his. "I thank you, Miss Ann, but Vicki is the real hero."

"I'm going to be sick." Before anyone could say anything to her, Vicki stood up and ran out of the house. Davis was right behind her. Ann got up, even with her ice pack plastered to her head, and put on a kettle of water.

"What do we do now?"

Good question, thought Leo, but he waited for Remy to answer Weston. There was a dead man in their house. Sure, it was self-defense, but someone was going to jail and from what he'd seen of the goings on here, that wasn't a good idea. They needed every man or woman they could get. Besides, having Vicki in a jail cell with her power could be dangerous for a lot of stupid people.

"We bury him in the back yard."

Weston nodded, and before Leo could point out that was almost as dumb of an idea as putting Vicki in jail, a young woman came crashing into the room with a baby in her arms.

Leo had been a fifth grade teacher for a long time. And being single and sort of good looking, he had been flirted with a great deal during parent/teacher meetings and after school events. And in all that time, children had been…little children had been around him. But he had never had the occasion to hold one. But he was suddenly holding Catherine's.

The kid looked at him with the darkest eyes he'd ever seen. Dark chocolate, he thought, and it was his favorite way to have the confection. The baby's eyes looked like he was older than his few weeks. His head full of equally dark hair seemed so soft that Leo ran his fingers over it to find that he'd been wrong. It was much softer than he could have ever thought. And while he was at it, he ran his fingers gently over his little chubby cheeks to have him take his finger into his tight fist. Leo was unprepared for the emotion that came with such a simply thing.

"It's wonderful, isn't it?" He looked up at Jarvis, who was standing over him. Looking back at the child, he could see that the baby had turned to the voice of the other man and was smiling at him. "Every time I look at him I want to snuggle him to me and keep him there. And the first time he smiled at me, I nearly wept."

Leo started to hand him back, but Jarvis declined. "He's your son. He'd probably feel better with you."

"Carter. His name is Carter. And even though he's not of my blood, he's my son. And you look to me like you could use a little of his special kind of magic." Jarvis looked over at Ann and Catherine. "They're telepaths. Both of them. And I would imagine that Carter will be as well. That's what the father, Catherine's father, wanted them for. He thought she could control people with her mind and get him all kinds of money in the process."

"That man?" Jarvis nodded and said nothing else. "He hurt Ann badly. Will she heal like the rest of this house can?"

"No. She's too human to heal like that." Jarvis looked at him. "You don't either. Why is that?"

"I don't know. I can heal faster, a good deal faster than other people can. But it's not instantaneous. But then I'd been very ill for a while before coming here." He had been nearly dead before leaving the hospital. In fact, he was pretty sure that someone had called the undertaker that morning. "I was healed by Hector. He said I was too good a man to be lost to such an illness. I wish that he'd left me alone."

"You'd rather be dead than here holding my son?" Leo didn't like the question, nor the implications that he was a pussy. But Jarvis laughed, and he looked up at him. "What will you do when you're in the middle of a fight with one of these guys? Will you let the malefactor kill you? Or will you stand and fight with them?"

"I won't leave anyone to die by those things. I've seen enough of their work." Jarvis nodded and looked at Ann, who was pulling things from the cabinets. It looked like she was planning to bake. "I don't want to be here either. This is not where I should be."

"None of us thought we'd be here. But had Catherine not come here with her mom, I would have lost them both. All three of them, as a matter of fact. That man would have killed them because they'd not be able to do what he wanted. Davis had cancer before coming here. I'm not sure what kind but, like you, he was dying. Remy was on a battlefield when Hector approached him. He, from what I've heard, had a long pike through his chest and would have died there without Hector." Jarvis took the baby when he started to fuss. "You think about what you're going to be doing, the lives you're going to save by being here, and then think about the people you would have left behind had you died then. Was there anyone there, one single person that might have benefited from your final breath?"

"I was going to be married." Jarvis told him he was sorry for that. "It's not your fault, but she decided that having me 'cramp her style' would have been too much for her to bear. Death till us parted wasn't really what she would have signed on for."

"Fuck her." He started to stand and tell him to fuck off, but the man only smiled. "You want to hit someone, go down to the gym and work off some of your anger with Remy. He's fucking scary big. Or Vicki. I'm sure she'd go a few rounds with you." Leo asked why not him. "Me? I'm much too pretty to let you beat on my face."

Leo laughed for the first time in days, maybe even weeks. He looked around the room and the people there. They were not a bad group. Just...just not what he'd thought he'd be with at this point in his life.

The grave only took about two hours to dig. He and Vicki were partners digging side by side for a time, then Davis and Remy. Skylar was out with them, but she was more of a lookout. They were burying the man, Wally Hathaway. It was thought that if anyone dug him up, they'd leave his grave open for the animals to take care of. This man was not at all liked.

"I'm not in a good place." Vicki only huffed at him. He was pretty sure she'd said something else, but he chose to ignore it rather than have her repeat what he thought she said. "I've had some major changes in my life that I wasn't happy with."

He stopped digging when she did and looked at her. "You weren't happy with them. I see. And you think that as a nurse, I'm thrilled to death to have taken a man's life. Yeah, he was a bastard, but I killed him with my bare hands. And every day, I kill even more people…well, what were once people. So if you don't mind me saying so, fuck off to you not being in a good place. We'll have a pity party for you when this is done."

"Christ, you're a hard ass. Anyone ever told you that before?" She stared at him. "I was ready to die. I was more than ready. My body had been…it wasn't easy going from so sick every day that I needed someone to keep me doped up to feeling like I could take over the world."

"Get over yourself. All of us here have been in a shitty place." She started digging as she continued. "I'm sorry that you were sick. Sorrier still that someone did something to you against your will. But you're here now, so either get over it or move on. We have enough to deal with without you mucking it up."

He wanted to be pissed. Take the shovel in his hands and hit her in the head with it. But the longer he stared at her, thinking of all the things he could do to her, the more he realized she was right. He was in a shitty mood. He wasn't instantly happy, not even feeling better about what was done to him, but he did know that being mad at this woman was going to get him hurt. Not by her mate, but her. She'd take him down a few pegs, break a few bones, and not think a thing about it.

As he made his way back to the house, feeling tired and sore, he said nothing to anyone but let them get ahead of him. Remy, however, slowed and was walking beside him as they entered the main part of the yard.

"Are you all right? I mean, you've made no bones about being here, but I don't want anyone here that is going to cause trouble." Leo looked at the man. Here was a man that he could like. A no nonsense sort of man that would do anything for you if you were only to ask. "I'm serious."

"As am I when I tell you that while I'm angry and upset with what has been done, like most things in life, I'll get over them. But as for trouble, you won't have any out of me. I'm…let's just say that I'm all right with my life for the moment." Remy stared at him, then nodded once and put out his hand. Leo stared at it, then at the man. "If you don't mind, I'm a little too sore right now to have you change something else about me."

Remy laughed. "I can understand that. Every time that Hector came around, for a while there anyway, I was terrified that the man was going to hurt me again. But I think for now, we're what we need to be. At least I hope. We're finding out things daily. You will too, I think."

"I'm sure you're right. Like today." He looked around and pulled his shirt off over his head. There on his hip and side were the most intricate tattoos Remy had ever seen. And he was still trying to figure out what it was. Remy had him turn for him.

"I think it's a dragon." Leo tried to look at him but from his angle it was nearly impossible. But he did notice that today it was up under his shoulders and lower on his hip. "You think you can change into one?"

"Christ, I hope not. What the hell would I do as a dragon?" Many things popped into his mind, most of them having very little to do with him resting under a tree while he napped. "You really don't think that's what is going to happen to me, do you?"

"I honestly have no idea. Everything about this situation is new to us. We're sort of playing this by ear." Leo nodded but didn't go into the house. Instead, he looked up at the sky. Could he really change into a dragon and fly the skies?

Chapter 7

His body hurt in more places than he knew that he had. By now, at least hours ago, he should have not just been healed but well on his way to going back to the compound and killing the fucking bitch. What had she hit him with? And where the hell had she come from?

"What the hell happened to you?" He could no longer hold the shape of his monster, so Master turned to look at Ward, and was surprised to see Dolin with him. Dolin looked as if he'd aged several times his known age. Master almost felt sorry for him. But feeling sorry for anyone but himself was too much today.

"Why was I not told of the weapon they have in that woman? She nearly took my life from me the day before yesterday." Dolin sat down on something on his end, and Master did the same. It was too hard for him to maintain this facade, so he didn't even try. "You said they would be easy to kill. You told me that once they were gone, all of them would be easy to control. That was a lie."

"What woman? You mean that mate of Rembrandt? I know of no such weapon that they have." Ward looked at Dolin. "Do you know anything about this?"

"I'm not talking of that bitch Skylar. I mean the new one. The one that smells of the fucking trees and something sweet, a newcomer to their group." Both men looked confused. Then Master remembered that they'd had no more contact with the stupid beings since Hector had defected. "She is tall, too skinny, and has a marking on her face and arms. She also smells of earth."

"Earth?" Dolin stood up and began to pace. "Hector said that there would be twelve of them to help battle against us. Are there any more men there? Perhaps one of them could have harmed you and you missed it."

His beast rose up. Not entirely because he was still too weak, but both of them shied back, even though he could no more harm them than they could him. Not unless he went back to their realm or they actually came here, which he doubted would ever happen under the current circumstances.

"I know when a woman raises her magic against me. And she did. There are only the two men there that are a threat to me. I will kill any more that come within miles of that place." He tried to think if there was anyone there when he'd been there, and all he could think was the woman. She had tried to kill him and had nearly succeeded. "I shall require more of the magical stones. There are a few stones here, empty of their magic, of course, but you can...why are you saying no? I need them."

"There's a problem with the magic. I...we never actually made it before, and since Hector has left us, things have not gone well." Dolin stopped moving around the room and stared at him as he continued, "We have nothing left. And the people of the lab, our lab, are leaving us faster daily. Not by choice, but we are being told they are dying. All of them. The blood of the dead has been spread to more of the people than we'd thought. Someone is killing them, and it's not us this time."

"Then I would suggest that you find out who it is and put a stop to them. Is that so hard for you to figure out?" Ward shook his head this time, saying that they couldn't find the person. "Are you telling me that you're no longer ridding your planet of the surplus of people there, but that someone else is doing it for you? You said that it would only be the ones that are draining our resources. You both told me by the time the fight on this realm was complete all that would be left on your end would be more than enough to serve us. We cannot start fresh at this point. People should have been kept trained. Why have you not trained others in his job? What are you doing there? And not working to fix this problem?"

"Hector didn't give us notice when he left, in case you forgot. We thought him grieving and never thought to go and get his notes when we tried to kill him. And when we read over his notes…none of us are able to figure out what the hell he was saying. His handwriting is all wrong, like he was writing in another language or something." Ward took a deep breath to apparently calm himself. But Master was too pissed himself to care at this point. "You'll have to take your time in healing on your own. I don't know what else to tell you."

"You might as well tell him the rest." Dolin only nodded toward him when he looked at Ward. "We're going to hear about it if we don't."

Master wanted to tell them to leave him. Dolin only nodded again when Master shook his head. He didn't want to know what else. Because surely what they had told him was the worst.

"Two of the orders we had have cancelled. They have decided that working with us is no longer a viable option. They have seen, apparently, what we have been dealing with on this other realm."

Master could only think of all the work he'd done so far for this. All the time and effort that he'd put in with the promise of a large payoff. His temper seemed to be growing with each beat of his heart, with every breath he took. But as he tried to calm his beast, tell him it would be fine, the pain was nearly unbearable. Master knew that losing control now would serve no purpose but to make him weaker. The men he was angry with were not going to feel his wrath anyway, so it would be a huge waste of his spent energy.

He felt the blackness that had plagued him of late take him, and knew there was little to nothing he could do to keep it at bay right now. He was too weak, too hurt to do anything but let it slide over his body and take him under.

When Master woke some time later, he knew that several hours had passed. The day was gone now and the sky was as black as his beating heart. Master smiled at his description of himself. He was sure that his heart, a dark and hard place anyway, was just as he'd said. Black as pitch.

"It would serve them right if I were to ride above their compound and toss fire upon them." Of course, he knew for a fact that it wouldn't work. Whoever had put the magic around the place had taken that precaution into account as well.

His wounds were deep this time. Looking down at them, it nearly made him ill to think just how close to his heart, black or otherwise, she'd come. Her magic had burned through his own magic until there was nothing left to keep him whole. And the fact that she'd done it at all was still burning into him. Did she not realize that he would rule her soon?

Master supposed it was very arrogant of him to think along those lines. The humans and these creatures that Hector had created to help the earth were not going to go down easy. He wondered at what point Hector had given them the extra powers. It had to be soon after they had gathered together. Because before that, Master had had no problems at all in turning the humans and killing off the others like Rembrandt. And there had been many others over the years since the day in the field where Rembrandt had been changed.

Over the decades there had been hundreds of the same type of man as Rembrandt. In fact, there had been more than a thousand of them created the day that Rembrandt had been. Even Master had thought of joining the fight, but he'd been more inclined to join Ward and Dolin than what he considered a lost cause with Hector's group of men.

Master sometimes forgot that Hector was there with them at the beginning, or so he'd been told. That Hector alone had been responsible for making and controlling the creatures that had been a part of their world.

But he'd killed all of Hector's warriors. Master would destroy these too, he'd no doubt of that. Every time that he'd heard one of the others talk about a new man that could turn the tides, he'd go and hunt the man down and kill him. Always leaving Remy, knowing that someday he'd come back to find him and tell him just what he'd done.

"That was a disappointment." Master frowned when he thought of the look in Remy's face when he'd told him what he'd done to his wife and children. He had expected him to sob. To cry out of the injustice of it all. But he'd not done either of those things. He'd been angry, yes that was true, but not the type of anger that Master had been hoping for. Remy always was a spoil sport.

Master went deeper into his cave. He would not have been happy for Ward or Dolin to see his new home, but then he was pretty sure that they could see as little of where he lived as he did with them. The big roaring fire was the only thing that he'd been able to make without making himself ill again. And it kept him very warm.

The bodies of the two men that had happened upon him were roasting over it. Master had had human before, and while it was good in some ways, he really didn't care for the taste. But it helped him heal, helped him in ways now that nothing else would. And there would be nothing else.

Master thought of the money. Two orders couldn't be that bad, could it? There were millions of beings that used the same stone they had for magic. Where else did they think they were going to get such stones if not from them? Unless Hector was going behind their backs and selling it at a discount rate. That would be so like him.

Poking at the meat, he grinned. No, that would be very unlike Hector. The man could barely make enough money to keep his family, and seemed to be so happy about it. Going to someone to deal with them was out of the question. He would wet himself if he had to even try.

Hector was a stupid man despite his abilities in the lab. He'd never go to someone in order to cheat another. It wasn't in his nature. Master prided himself on reading people, and Hector was a pussy. A whiny pussy.

~~~

Dolin sat down. He was nervous, Ward could tell, but it was time to cut ties with the fool on earth and move on to someone that could be controllable. And Benton no longer was. He sat in his own chair and waited. Sooner rather than later, Dolin would start to speak. It was much sooner than he'd thought it would be.

"Do you think he suspects anything?" Ward stretched his legs out in front of him without answering. "If he figures out what we're doing, he's going to come here and kill all of us. I know it has to be done, but it's dangerous. He has a nasty temper, you know. And as much as I'd like to have him kill the others, I do worry about him coming here."

"Of course it's dangerous. We knew that from the first. But Benton is beginning to play by his own rules, and that is going to get us nowhere. You heard what the buyer said. If we're having this much trouble controlling one man, then why should they expect us to come through for them? I'm not going to go under before we even get this thing going."

"It was a big blow to our plans to have them back out." Ward nodded at Dolin. "When do you meet with the others? The ones in that realm? The sooner we can get some answers and some money, the better I'll feel."

"Tomorrow. They're supposed to be looking for a candidate to bring here so that we can change him on our own. He'll have to be semi stupid, I think, but smart enough to work himself out of tight things when necessary." Dolin asked how many they were going to bring here. "Four or five, I think. Once they're here, we can figure out who we're going to change. I'm really glad you found the notes that Hector left behind. Now if we could only find someone who can decipher them."

The notes had been found in his home, under the bed that his wife had died in. Ward had only found them because he'd sold the mattress to someone and had been there when they'd pulled it out. The books, five in all, were bundled in an old baby blanket tucked up under the frame of the bed. There had been other things as well; a magazine that featured Hector on the cover, a wedding picture of someone he had no clue who they were, and a piece of turquoise. It had burned him badly when he'd picked it up, not having a clue what Hector had done to it to make it so different.

"Did you ever figure out what the turquoise was used for?" Ward shook his head and said that he'd never even see the stone until then. "I've only just heard about it. The humans wear it around their necks and fingers as jewelry. Whatever for, I can't imagine. But they are an odd bunch of beings. I, for one, will be glad when they're all gone."

"I have never even spoken to one directly, other than the ones we brought here. Surely they aren't the true nature of them, are they?" Dolin looked shocked, and Ward had no way to set his mind at ease. "If that is the case, then it is small wonder we're having so much trouble there. Why would they adorn themselves with such oddities?"

"Why indeed?" Ward felt a wave of sadness wash over him. It was happening less and less these days, but it was still there, his loss of his best friend. Mary had meant the world to him. And now he was going to make them all pay for her death. "I've been trying to figure out where Hector is. He told you once that we'd never be able to breach the compound. Do you suppose that now that he's there, we could? It would certainly make things easier on us if we could bring him back here and make him tell us what to do."

Ward didn't think that was going to happen, even if they were able to breach the compound walls. If that was where he was. Hector had been hiding from them for a while now, and Ward had no doubt that he knew a great deal more about them than they did him. Like those fucking books. He'd done that on purpose. Writing them, then filing them away so that neither of them could read it.

"Doubtful. It was our blood that made the monsters in that realm. And it is that alone that keeps us from entering the compound. It might be where Hector is too, but we've no one inside to help us find out. I wonder at times if he never really trusted us. I mean, when you think of all the precautions he'd come up with to ensure that he was the only one that could read his notes. He also changed and watched over that Rembrandt person without letting us know what he'd been up to. Of course we had our secrets too, but his were more to give himself gain, not to help us all."

Ward pointed out that they'd done the same thing. "I know what you mean, however. He was and still is so single-minded about his plans. It was as if he knew that soon we'd be turning our backs on him. Do you suppose at any time he figured it out? Or was this all lucky guesses on his part?"

"I've no idea." Ward got up to get him a drink. It was getting harder and harder to get help these days. And he was suspicious about the amount of deaths being reported to him daily. But if they weren't really dead, where were they? Not in town. The place was eerily quiet nowadays. Store fronts were closed up. There were no children at the schools. And very few of the people employed even showed up to work anymore. He had been reduced to making his own bed. If not dead, then if he found them, they would wish that they were.

"Back to Benton." Ward sat down while Dolin continued. "He said that one of the women hurt him. And while I know that he's injured, what do you suppose really happened? Do you think that Rembrandt has gotten smarter and got the jump on him?"

"Did you see the wound?" Ward shivered when he thought of what it had looked like. "I thought for sure that we were going to see his backbone, the wound was so deep. And it looked as if he'd been burned. The gunshot wounds on his body were bad enough, but that looked like someone had touched him with some sort of hot fire or magic. Who would have that much power to hurt him like that?"

No one that he knew of. Rembrandt certainly couldn't, not that he was aware of. But things were going on that they were not privy to, and that irked him more than the books and hidden things in Hector's house. Things he'd not even told Dolin about.

After the other man left, Ward made his way to Mary's place. He'd had it made especially for him. Of course, her body was not here; they didn't bury their dead like some species did, but burned them in a crematory. Things were better that way, he had thought at the time, but now…now he would give anything to be able to go to where she might be resting and talk to her.

"I love Dolin to no end, but there are times when I would simply like to hit him." He laughed because it was something he'd said to her countless times. "Things are not going as we had planned. Rembrandt is out of control. Not just because he killed you, but because of the way things are going on that realm. He is killing more of the creatures than we can create. I don't think he's aware of that yet, but when he figures it out, he'll be relentless in his efforts to end what we've started. And at this rate, we will have less of them than we need to take over the world. That would be costly to us all."

The flowers that he'd planted himself were blooming now. Things on this realm did better than any other place he'd been. Flowers, such as this one, would bloom for months on end, then go dormant for a few weeks only to rise up and be twice as big. It was perfect for his little garden.

"The things that I told you about the other day, I'm still no closer to figuring out what the use of them are than I was before. If only I could read the books." He sighed heavily. "I know that the answers are there, but what they are alludes me. Do you suppose he made it up on his own and there will never be any hope of us figuring it out without him?"

A woman walked by his little cove, but he said nothing. It wasn't like him to be unfriendly, but of late he'd not wanted anything to do with anyone. Even Dolin seemed to get on his last nerve. And Ward found himself out here more often than not. He was no longer happy.

Losing Mary had taken a great toll on him. He'd loved her, yes, but she'd been his friend too. And Dolin's. Ward had used Mary to bounce ideas off of; her plans, at times, were better than his, and when she took him to her bed, not often but enough, he felt as if he were king of the world already, and would bask in her love making long after he was sent home.

"The turquoise is something important. I'm not sure what, but there you have it. I know that it's important somehow, but not sure what. And Benton is hurt again. The man has served his purpose to us. As I have told you before, it's time to get rid of him. But how is the big question. Perhaps if we leave him there on that earth, Rembrandt will finish him off for us." He looked at the small picture of Mary that he'd put out here several days ago, imagined her smiling at him with that look in her eyes. "You were right. Is that what you wanted to hear? You knew from the start that he was going to be our downfall, and we should have listened. Oh, to be back to the beginning and know what we do now. I would have done so many things as you suggested."

She'd told them both, countless times, to get rid of Hector. And to have someone watching over him at all times taking notes and learning the process. Mary had also suggested that they have someone training with him, someone to take over in the event that something happened to Hector. Well, nothing had happened, but there were more problems than he was sure Mary would have thought of too.

Ward sat there for several hours, mostly talking to his friend but resting too. His energy level was low of late. He'd even taken to only eating things he'd cooked himself, having some idea that it was his food that was making him so ill. But it turned out that he was still weak and that nothing seemed to help. Not even taking several naps during the day and going to bed early at night had helped him. There was something wrong with him, and he was very careful with everything until he figured out what it could be.

Standing up, he looked down at the little spot. There were stains in the dirt, wet ones. Going into his house, he stripped down and saw the blood on his legs and thighs. He knew what this was, knew that someone was poisoning him. Going to the door, he was going to confront Dolin, demand that he confess, but the man was already there, his own hands covered in blood.

"Someone is poisoning me. Is it you?" Ward shook his head and showed him the blood on himself. "What is this? We've been so careful all this time. What's happening that we're sick as well?"

"We didn't put the poison in the water. And even if we did, I never drink it." Dolin said that he didn't either. He was afraid of it. "The food I care for myself. And there is no help here in my house. I don't know what to think. We're not going to die, Dolin. We're going to figure this out."

"We're being poisoned. Someone wants us dead. But why?" Ward could think of any number of reasons why, but voiced none of them. Dolin had to be aware of the things they'd done, the people that they'd killed. "Who would do this? Who?"

As Dolin paced, Ward tried to think. The only thing that the two of them had done lately was go to the earth, about a week ago, to see to the other man. This man was trying to find a connection to the compound that he could use. Someone that could get in without being traced back to them. So far the only luck they'd had was an ex-husband of one of the household staff, who just happened to be Mary's sister. And they'd not heard from him in days.

"I think it's the earth." Ward looked at Dolin when he spoke. "Remember when that guy offered us that wine when we were there? It was nasty as crap, but we drank it. I think it was that. I think he gave us something to poison us."

"We had two glasses, if I remember. He told us that it would be a way to seal the deal. I don't remember...did he have food for us as well?" Dolin said that he didn't know. "Well, we can get better so long as we don't eat or drink any more of the poison. How he got any of it is beyond me."

The stone he'd found in the house kept circling around in his head. What had it been used for? Why did Hector even have it? Was it part of the formula that he'd been working on? It was in his pocket, he realized, and pulled it out. When he sat it on the table, Dolin pulled a similar piece and laid it there as well. He asked him where he'd gotten it.

"That man, Wainwright, gave it to me. He said it was a good luck charm." They both stared at the two stones. "You don't think that's making us sick, do you?"

Ward did. In fact, he was sure of it. He had no idea why, but he was nearly as positive as he was about his love for Mary that this thing had been the reason they were sick. He didn't touch the pieces, but shoved them into the trash bin next to his table. Picking it up, he threw the entire thing in the larger can in his kitchen. Whatever it was, whatever properties the stones had in them, Ward was sure they were never coming into contact with any part of him again.

"Go home. Drink lots of clean water. Boil it first so that there are no impurities in it. Eat only your own food that you cook and prepare. Don't let anyone give you anything that you don't know for sure is safe. And for the love of everything, stay away from earth. There are things going on there that we cannot control." Dolin stood up and nodded. He hesitated at the door before leaving.

"I thought it was you." Ward didn't say that he'd thought the same thing. He wanted to be the better man in this, even if he was sick too. "I'm sorry for that now. I was so afraid that I just knew it was you."

"We'll beat this. We just have to trust one another. From now on, we only trust each other." Dolin left him and Ward went to bathe. The blood had slowed now that he'd removed the small stone, and that reinforced his idea that that was what had caused it.

For some reason when poison entered their systems, they bled out slowly from their main arteries in their thighs. Nowhere else did they bleed. And Ward was well aware that there were a few other places that held bigger, thicker veins. Why the legs, he had no clue. But he wrapped the wounds in soft gauze and then lay down. He was going to beat this or know the reason why.

Chapter 8

Davis moved up behind the first group of monsters and killed three before they were even aware that he was nearby. While keeping an eye on Vicki, he made his way to the big building and then inside. Jake had said that a large group of the malefactors was inside. Davis looked up at Remy when he came from the other side of the building.

"Skylar is taking Vicki to the other exit. I don't think that these monsters are aware of the door as yet, but this whole thing might be a decoy. She is going to watch her." Davis nodded. Since she'd killed Ann's husband, Vicki had been extremely quiet. And she'd been spending a great deal of time out of doors, just sitting and staring off into space.

"I'm worried about her." Remy said he was as well. "When she's like that, it's all I can do not to go and dig up Hathaway and kill him again."

"I understand. Skylar said that she'd make sure that she got help. I have no idea what that might mean, but we're working on it. And so you know, Ann is going to talk to her tonight. Tell her just how she feels about her ex being dead."

That might help, Davis thought, but had no idea. When a man killed someone in the line of duty, they were put behind a desk. Then they saw a shrink for several weeks only to be put back on the job well before they were ready. He'd seen it countless times, and he was worried that Vicki being out here today was going to break her.

Leo came around the other side of the building covered in blood. Not his own, they could both see, but in the blue blood of the malefactors. He was another person that Davis was worried about. While he wasn't as bitter as he'd seemed when he'd first gotten here, he was still moody. He, too, had been spending time outside, but his had been working with Ann and Margarita. He was teaching them some moves with a knife. Davis thought it was a wonderful idea.

"We go in together, then split up. I don't want any of us to go to the next floor until we're sure we're all right." Remy looked around the big warehouse that they'd just entered. "We'll go through here killing what we can, then meet here when we're done. The girls are going to watch the outside and let us know if there is a mass exodus. Got it?" Both he and Leo said they did, and they split into different directions.

It was an open plan of a building, but the view was blocked by large wooden crates. Davis would have broken a few of them open in his days as a cop, just to make sure that there were no drugs or bodies in them, but not now. It always amazed him what a person would do to get to money or things that didn't belong to him, and the extreme measures he'd take to kill when someone tried to get it back.

Once, when he'd been a cop, Davis had come across a large container sitting by the side of the road. It had been tagged by someone a few days before as abandoned. Davis drove by it for three more days before he finally couldn't stand it any longer and got of his cruiser to check it out. The smell of death nearly made him get into his car and drive away. But he called it in, then waited for someone to come and give him the okay to open it. By then, well before they arrived with the clippers, he knew that the people inside had died.

There were fifty-three adults and ten children in the container. Buckets at each end had been used as toilets. That alone was enough to make a person sick, after being in the closed up container for days in the heat. But the way those people had been packed inside made him wonder if there had been any way to use the buckets without shuffling herds of people around just to piss in one of them. But still they had managed somehow.

It had taken him a week of washing his uniform before he simply tossed it in the fire and burned it. The stench had been that bad. At times, when he got his holster or belt wet, he got a whiff of the smell, and his belly would roll with it.

Today he was a different sort of cop. He killed indiscriminately and did so daily. Some days he'd take out as many as two hundred of the malefactors without speaking to a one of them. Today, this job made him a protector, a different sort of serve-and-protect kind of cop. And Davis thought he was a better man for it. Certainly a better cop.

He could see Leo coming around one of the containers. Davis nearly called out his location to him when someone moved out in front of him. It took Davis several seconds to realize that it was Vicki's brother. Focusing on the two of them, he listened in to what was being said.

"All you have to do is get me in the house. The rest will be all me. I need to see my sister. She and I have some things to talk about." If Leo said anything, Davis didn't hear it, but Randall continued as if he had. "I really don't care how you do it. But I'm willing to pay you big time for your help. What's you say?"

"I said no thanks. And your sister? I have a feeling that she's no more in a hurry to see you than I am." As Leo tried to move around Randall, the younger man shoved him against the container. "I'm reasonably sure that you want to back the fuck off me about now. I'm in no mood to get into a pissing contest with you and more than that, I have no time to explain why I had to kill you to the people I'm working with. Piss off."

Again Leo tried to move around him, but either Randall was on something or he was just that stupid. Both, Davis figured, when Randall got up in Leo's face. Leo shoved him back so hard that he hit the container, a metal one this time, and it moved a good four or five inches across the floor. As Randall lay there unconscious, Davis walked toward him.

"He wants his sister." Davis nodded and looked down at the man. "I'm assuming it's Vicki and not Skylar. I wouldn't fuck with either of them, but he seems to think that someone wants them not just for their mind. They're pretty enough, but I have a feeling that either one of them could kick my ass even as buff as I am now."

"Count on it." Davis leaned down and reached into Randall's pants. Removing his wallet, a stone fell out of his pocket. It was the roundest turquoise he'd ever seen. Putting it in his own pocket, he looked in the wallet. "Eleven dollars. No credit cards and no identification. What do you suppose that means? Just the other day I saw him with a guy who gave him a wad of cash. What do you suppose he's done with it?"

Leo reached down and tore Randall's sleeve without a word. There they were...track marks from his wrist to his elbow in a long line that followed his vein. And most of them were as fresh looking as today. So now he knew the reason for Randall's lack of cash. But what he didn't know was who the man was who'd paid him, or why he was buying Vicki.

Malefactors were moving into the warehouse in front of him. Remy was coming to them from the same direction, and Davis stood up with Leo. They watched them move. It looked as if they were being drained even as they shuffled across the floor. Two of them fell face first on the concrete, and the rest walked over the fallen ones as if they weren't there. Davis pointed them out to Remy when he was standing next to him.

"Come look at this." Remy led them around the malefactors. The beings ignored them completely, walking around in a daze, bumping into each other. "I was looking from room to room when I noticed this sound coming from this part of the building. I called in Skylar and Vicki because you two were dealing with the asshole over there, and I didn't think it would be good if Vicki saw him."

Davis wondered how Remy knew but said nothing for now. They'd told him about the exchange, but as far as he knew, Remy had no idea what the man looked like. But then Remy opened the door and they looked into the room where both Vicki and Skylar were.

"Christ. What the hell is that?" Remy walked around it with them as Leo spoke in hushed tones. "Is this some sort of battery?"

"Yeah, I think that might be what it is." Remy walked to the back of it and pointed to a long wire coming from the back. "I've been tempted to pull this, just to see what it is, but I'm sort of afraid of it. I mean, for all we know, this might be the only reason there aren't seven million of these things running around and not the several thousand that we're dealing with."

"Do you think Hector would know?" Vicki walked up to Davis and put her arms around him. After a quick kiss, she turned to Skylar. "How hard would it be to go and get him and bring him here? I mean, if you were to fly?"

"You can fly." Davis still hadn't gotten the hang of it, and was shaking his head even as Skylar pointed at him. "Yes you can. I've seen you do it."

"You've seen me fumble with it a great deal. What if I drop him? Or worse yet, fall to the ground with him in my arms." He shook his head again as he continued, "You go and get him, bring him here, and we'll get this fixed. Then as soon as we get back to the compound, I'll let you give me a lesson. Deal?"

Skylar looked at Remy, who was laughing. At his nod, Skylar went out of the building. Davis saw her shadow as she lifted from the ground. Davis knew he had to get the hang of this flying crap, and soon. So did Vicki. Though, to be honest, she was better at it than him.

In ten minutes, Skylar returned. Hector was smiling until he looked at the device. Twice he walked around it before coming to stand near the cords that Remy had been tempted to pull. He reached down and pulled the plug out of the wall, and the response was immediate.

The malefactors seemed to come alive. Not just animated but literally alive. Their color went from the faded hue to real color, their clothing—which always included a tee-shirt with a single pocket — disappeared, and what was more than likely their own clothing before the change came into focus. But the biggest change was their faces. Not only did they not all look alike, they appeared lost and confused. One of them looked at him and spoke.

"Where am I?" Davis didn't answer but watched the man's face. "I was on my way to work. Something…I had an accident and…. Where am I?"

Davis told him. "This is a warehouse near the riverfront. I'm assuming that you had been hurt pretty badly to end up here. When did you have this accident? Do you remember the date?" The man said no. "I'm sorry, but for a while now, the monsters have been converting humans into killing machines."

"Have I?" Davis told him more than likely. "I'm a good man. A husband, father. I would never do such a thing. Never."

He started to fade again, but this time he looked like he was aware. If not totally, then enough to know that this was something he wasn't going to live with. Walking to the wall, he looked at the machine and pulled open one of the panels on it. Before anyone could stop him, he put his hand inside of it and screamed.

The power that surged through the man was more than Davis had thought it would be. When he was dead, long before he let go of the wires, two more people came to do the same thing. When the power — or whatever had been stored in the machine — had diminished, they saw that the other malefactors were all down, apparently dead.

~~~

Vicki rode in the back of the car to the compound. There were ninety-three dead malefactors laying in the building, and all of them had been killed the moment that men—three in all—had pulled out the wiring harness and had set it to their chests. It had been a group hug, it seemed, to die together. They hadn't just died but had blown apart right before their eyes. And the only reason that they knew how many had died was the head count. The heads had rolled away from each of the bodies as if they had wanted no part of the rest of them.

As soon as they entered the house, she asked Davis to come with her. She needed him. The bedroom door was barely closed when she was naked and kissing him. He pulled her back only long enough to pick her up and take her to the bed.

This wasn't going to be love making—not even sex—but a fucking. She needed to be fucked—and hard. As soon as he flipped her over to her belly and pulled her ass up to his cock, she knew that he understood what she needed.

His cock filled her nearly as soon as she laid her head onto the bed. His fingers, usually so gentle and soft, gripped her hips hard enough that she knew that he was leaving marks. But it wasn't enough. She needed more. As his hands moved up her back, trailing up her spine, she nearly cried out when his fingers curled into her hair and jerked her head back. The pain was incredible.

"Come and I'll hurt you." She knew he was going to anyway, but the thought of not being able to come when she wanted made her wetter, her body tighter for the release. "You think I'm kidding you? Come and you will hurt, Vicki."

Her body reacted to his words like he'd told her to come. Her release was so powerful that she saw stars behind her eyelids, her heart felt twisted in her chest, and her pussy ached for more. When he leaned over her, tearing into her shoulder, she came again, tightening around him until he couldn't move. Twice he bit down into her flesh, bringing her every time until she fell to the bed. But Davis only pulled from her and turned her over, bringing her legs up and wide while he buried his face over her pussy.

He devoured her. Eating her not with his lips and tongue but with his fangs, digging them into her over and over until she begged him to stop, no longer able to come and stay conscious. But he didn't stop. He didn't even slow in his all-consuming hunger for her. His fingers sliding into her ass made her scream out again as he ate her over and over. Still, he devoured her until he sat up on his knees and looked down at her.

When she sat up, his cock was thick with need, its crown so dark she wondered if he was close to exploding. She reached for him, but her hand was smacked away as he fisted his cock and held his balls. When he came, his cock squirting his juices all over her, Vicki rubbed it into her breasts, licked it from her lips, and moaned when he slid into her. This time he was the gentle man that she loved.

He took her to her peak twice as he made love to her. Tears streamed down her face as his love seemed to pour from him into her. Holding him to her, keeping his body inside of her, Vicki came with a scream, her body bowing up so hard that she felt him nearly slide out of her. His own release was not far behind hers as she fell back to the bed, and his fangs sank into her throat as he emptied himself once more.

When he rolled to his back, taking her with him, Vicki let her tears fall. She was in love with this man, there was no doubt about it, but she wasn't sure how much more she could take of this lifestyle. When he spoke, breaking her from her dark thoughts, she looked up at him and asked him to repeat himself.

"I said I saw your brother today. He was at the warehouse. Leo actually spoke to him. Randall wanted him to bring you to him." She asked him what Leo had said. "He hit him."

Vicki stared at him, shocked. First because he'd sounded so amused by what he'd said, and secondly because her brother was really trying to get her to come to him. Then the absurdity of the entire thing hit her.

"Mother fuck. I'm so dumb." He told her she wasn't and kissed her nose. "Thanks, but I am. I'm laying here with you feeling all sorry for myself because a bunch of people got killed. I had nothing to do with it. I mean, a few of them I did, but nothing more than that. And those people were going to kill us. Then my brother steps in and tries to get me. No, that's not right, he tries to sell me."

"He used the money for drugs. He has track marks all over his arms." Vicki knew her brother was a cokehead and wondered now why she didn't think about him selling her for money. He'd done more for drug money.

"When I was working at the hospital one night, I was called to ER. I had all sorts of thoughts as to why I had been asked to come down. All of them centered on my mom and what might have happened to her. She'd been working at the clinic for about two weeks then, and it wasn't in the best sort of neighborhood. But it was Randall. He'd been brought in." She got up and walked to the window, dressing herself in thick sweatpants and sweatshirt as she went, suddenly very cold. "They had strapped him down with leather ties that are sometimes used to hold down a combative person like he was. Randall had already hit one of the nurses, and the police were asking me questions. None of which I knew the answers to. All the while he's begging me to let him go, it's all a mistake."

"It usually is to them." Davis sat up. She noticed that he had dressed too, in the same manner she had, as if he too were cold. "I did a lot of calls where someone in the house was violent because they couldn't get a fix. What did he do to you?"

"Hit me. Almost as soon as they let him go, he doubled his fist and hit me. I had nineteen stitches in my cheek and another ten in my arm. They were letting him go to take him to jail. There was little to nothing they could do for him since he had refused treatment." She looked out the window again. "I never trusted him again, and avoided him as much as possible. And did a good job except for when he would catch me off guard somewhere. The security staff at the hospital knew that if he came on the premises that he was to be arrested and I was not to be called unless he was dead. I washed my hands of him that day, and since."

"Until now." She turned to look at him again. "We're going to have to deal with him. Sooner rather than later. He's going to keep at you until he finds someone that will help him. And we can't let him have you. I love you and need you here with me."

"I should just blast him." Davis grinned at her. "I was kidding. Sort of. I'm not sure what I could do if it came down to me and him. I don't...I guess I could hurt him if I needed to, but it would be hard."

"You could do it. I'm sure of it. He's low on your list right now." She asked him what kind of list he was talking about. "When I was a cop, there was so much going on all the time. Drug deals going down, jaywalkers, car jackings. Right within feet of one another. I would have to have a list. Drug deals were going to happen, nearly a fact of life. But if it was to a kid, it shot right to the top of the list. Same with the jackings. A sweet old woman was higher than some jackass that was asking for it to drive a nicer car in that neighborhood. Did they deserve to be hurt? No. But there was no way I could be everywhere at once. Some things, like the jaywalkers, never made the cut. It was all I could do not to go insane trying to be a great cop in a crime-infested war zone. So I had a list. It kept me from killing the wrong person, namely me. I even had one when I was diagnosed with cancer. It was just a way to deal with what I could control."

Standing at the window, she thought about what had brought her here. Not to this room, but to this place. So much had happened in a short amount of time. More than she'd ever dreamed possible really.

"I'm in love with you. I never thought I'd love anyone. I guess it was my upbringing that did that. But you're very amazing, and I'm a better human because of you." He got up and came to her. When he wrapped his arms around her, Vicki felt love like it was a warm blanket coming from him. "I hope we can finish this soon. I'd very much like to get on with our lives."

"We will. In the meantime, we have to work on my flying. You have it down, but I'm still knocking things over...and people. I hate it when I knock someone down." He kissed her ear. "Let's go out and see what sort of damage I can do out there."

They were nearly out the door when Ann called them back. She showed them the new panic button that had been installed, as well as asking to speak to Vicki alone. Davis left them, and Ann hugged her almost as soon as the door shut behind him.

"You saved my life. And that of my daughter and grandchild. I can't tell you how terrified I was when he hit me." Vicki tried to tell her it was all right. "No, it isn't. He was bent on killing me, and you saved me. I'll never forget that. Not so long as I live, and every time I kiss my grandson, I'll think of you saving me."

"I don't want you to do that. You should just be happy that one of us was up here when he came." Ann nodded and hugged her again. Vicki leaned against the counter. "My brother is looking for me. Did Mom tell you?"

"Yes. She said he was out there looking for a quick fix that would get you hurt if he found you." Vicki nodded. Leave it to her mom to cut to the chase. "I want you to know that he won't get by me. Not with that button there."

"Just be careful. He and Leo tangled today. He's a mean ass when he's high. And he doesn't care if you're a woman or not." Vicki started out and stopped. "Do you know how to use a gun? He's human, so it will work on him. I'll have someone show you if you don't."

"I can use one. Tell them I want one and that I want a place to practice. Your mom and I will take lessons if necessary." Vicki went out with Davis and told him what was going on.

"I'll train them both. It would be my pleasure. And that's a good idea that they both carry. It might be the difference between life and death for a lot of people." She agreed with him. "Now. Spread your wings, my dear, I want to learn how from the best."

They were out in the yard for nearly two hours. Skylar and Remy had joined them earlier on in their work out, and the four of them worked together to get the taking off down pat. Vicki could do that, but it was the landing that messed her up. She couldn't seem to turn in midflight to land on her feet. Usually, she was on her head when she set down. But it was fun to get out of the house and not think about what they were doing. She decided to make this a regular thing, to get out of the building and do something fun. They were all working way too hard and needed to have some fun or explode.

Chapter 9

"What do you mean, the power has been turned off? That's not possible. We have it hooked right into the wall." Dolin was getting angrier by the second. The man at the other end of the conversation was not telling him the truth. "I want you to go there and check again. The only people who knew about that grid was Ward, and he would not do something as stupid as that."

"I'm standing right next to the machine. All the parts have been burned up. The housing that puts off the waves has been destroyed, as well as the entire machine has been wrecked. There are enough of the creatures laying around, headless I might add, to make me think that one of them done it. There is evidence that one of them might have crawled up in the thing." Dolin wanted to scream. "Not to mention, there is some...I think it might be a message to you guys."

"Message?" He felt his blood chill when he heard the words. "Message of what sort? If it's in an envelope, then you have my permission to open it and read it."

"Nope. It's on the wall. And now that I'm standing back from it—the sucker is really big—I can see that it is to you and Mr. Ward. Let me see if I can get it all for you." There was a scraping sound as well as something falling over. It would be just Dolin's luck that the man would fall over and die before he got the information. "Okay, here we go. You want me to read it word for word or just give you the general idea?"

"Word for word if you please." It was hard to be polite, and Dolin was having a hard time just being civil to the man. "And do hurry. I'm late for something."

"Okay. 'Morons.' Then he has your name and Ward under it. Not very nice, is it?" Dolin was so close to hanging up the call and going to the scene himself that he had to grip the side of the couch to make sure that he didn't. "'I have destroyed your device. And so you know, Hector said that now that you've put one in, he'll know to look for them. He said you shouldn't waste your time; he will destroy them as fast as you build them. From now on we're going to be hunting for you.' Then at the end there's this little shaky line. Under it the word 'turquoise' is written. You know what that means?"

The phone fell from his hands. He looked at the piece of turquoise that had been in his robe pocket this morning when he'd slipped it on to go and talk to Mary. And then when he'd thrown it away, putting it in the outside can this time, he'd come into the house to find it on the counter. It was the same piece, he knew it. He'd been about to call Ward when this idiot called.

The machine had been built in the secret of the night. It was to bring the malefactors to the building, and the energy was funneled to his and Ward's homes. It was the only way now that they could charge up the stones that they were powering the lab with…with magic from the creatures it was made for. They were essentially supplying themselves with the power to create more of their kind. And it was the main reason they'd not been able to give any more to Benton. The man would suck them dry if they let him.

Dolin was still sitting there when Ward slapped him. It took Dolin a few seconds to realize that he might have been there for a while.

"What is it? I get this call from that fool you have on earth telling me that he thinks someone killed you. And when I get here you're in a trance." Dolin nodded but said nothing as Ward went on. "And did you send me that fucking stone again? This is not funny, Dolin. I'm not—"

He pointed to the one on his counter. Ward went to it but never touched it. Instead he put a bowl over it and came back to the couch. He didn't look any happier than Dolin felt. He told him about the machine.

"Hector did it?" Dolin nodded. "Why? What harm was it doing him for us to have it? It's not like we're taking the humans from them. Just using the energy that we need to make more. Doesn't he understand that?"

Dolin just stared at him. Ward could not be that stupid. Before he could tell him why it bothered Hector so much, Ward got up and put his stone that had been in a plastic Baggie under the bowl as well.

"Whatever this turquoise is, Hector is using it as well. It was on the message from, I'm assuming, Remy." Ward paled. "That was my reaction as well. We're going to have to do something about him. This has gotten well out of control. Is there anyone we can trust to go after him?"

"Not yet. I'm talking to one such person. He said that they owe him, whatever that means. I'm assuming that he thinks they've slighted him somehow." Dolin had no idea, but if the man wanted to help them out, then he was all for it. "He is demanding a million dollars to do it. Said he has needs." Dolin waited for him to tell him it was a joke, or at least tell him where he was going to get that kind of money. Since this thing with Hector, his money had been going to things that he thought would make his life better once they made it to earth.

"We don't have that kind of money. Not even with the money that was deposited for the first shipment. We've had needs as well." Boy, had they ever. Of the nearly five million in jewels and coin that they'd been given, only about a third of his portion was left. He'd gone through almost two million dollars in less time than it had taken them to set this thing up.

"I have most of my money left. No reason to spend it here when it would be nicer to have things, new things in the new world. We're still going to set up there, right? Live there?" Dolin nodded. How could Ward not have spent his money? But before he could ask, Ward continued. "Also, I took it upon myself to have someone look into houses for us. With that kind of money we can afford something on a grand scale. There will be plenty to choose from cheaply now that all the humans are gone."

"I should hope so since there will be no one there to gainsay us." Free was what he was hoping for. And with the money that was being left behind—hundreds of millions of dollars, he thought—they could live in style. "I was thinking we should narrow down our list of those we plan to take with us. We're going to need a staff and such."

Ward handed him a sheet of paper. "I've been thinking the same thing. I have ten names there. There were twenty-five, but as they are getting sick, my list has shortened."

They both looked at the bowl on the counter. "You think someone here is trying to kill us?"

"I don't know." But he had a feeling that it was Hector somehow. He had no idea how, but it was him. He was sure of it. "Perhaps someone is working with Hector. Making it so we get sick as well. I don't know anyone that would want us dead. We have given them so much, but you never know about some people. Maybe we should keep a closer eye on the people working with us."

Ward nodded. "I have been working from home. This is the only place that I come anymore. I've even taken to having my food delivered to me. Then I leave it in the hall for a while before I touch it. Even then it's with gloves. I'm so nervous about getting sick again."

It had taken them very little time to get over the poisoning, so little that Dolin wondered now if it was also a trick of the mind. There had been so many things going odd in the last weeks that he was beginning to doubt his sanity. He wasn't ill in the head, but there were things going on that made him think twice.

"Have you seen anything, heard anything in your home of late?" Ward looked confused. "It was just once, but I swear to you I heard someone screaming in my bedroom. Nearly made me fall all over myself getting there to look. Nothing like that?"

"No. I've been...now that you bring it up, I have noticed that my things are moved. I know it's not the cleaning person because she's not been there in weeks. But all the same, my books will be out of order. A chair just not right." Ward flushed. "I've taken to taking pictures of my rooms when I leave them and comparing them when I return. There is some movement."

So there was someone playing with them. But who? Neither of them went anywhere but to each other's houses. They didn't even go to the lab anymore because like Ward, Dolin had taken to working at home. Who would it be? Hector would have to know their schedules and be ready at a moment's notice to get there and out. Dolin wondered if they didn't have someone spying on them, reporting back to Hector when they left.

"I think I'm being paranoid." Dolin looked at Ward. "I have all these things running through my head. And all of them have spies or cameras looking in on us all the time. I think...why are we so afraid of Hector? What on earth could he have to hold against us? Surely our Mary passing is payment enough for his wife, don't you think? I mean, we've all lost someone in this. Move on, I say."

"Indeed." Ward had a good point. They had Hector's notes, all his lab equipment, and just recently they've gotten his computer opened. It was much like his notes in that no one could read them, but if they couldn't then neither could their competition. Nodding, Dolin decided to let go of this stuff and concentrate on getting things in the other world finished up so they could get paid.

"I'm going to have that man brought here. The one we talked about." Ward nodded and took out his little computer. He was forever taking notes, which, Dolin supposed, was a good thing and something that he should start doing. He was forever forgetting things. "When he is out of quarantine, I'll contact you and we'll get him set up for the transformation. He should be ready to do the work we need within a few weeks."

For the next several hours, they talked about work that needed done on the young human. He was perfect for what they needed, but they were both a little concerned about his intelligence. The man was not the smartest human they'd come across, but he did have the brawn to back up his work. There was also the amount of drugs he had in his system all the time. Dolin could almost taste them on him it was so strong.

As he left, Ward laughed about their earlier worries. "We're going to do just fine with this. In a few weeks, we're going to be on top of the world. Both worlds."

Dolin agreed and watched the man scurry home. As he put his hands in his pocket, he nearly fell backward. Pulling out the round, smooth stone, he could only stare at it in disbelief. Running to the bowl, he lifted it up and saw that not only was his missing, but Ward's was as well. Dolin would bet anything that Ward would find it in his pocket.

~~~

Hector was nervous. He'd never been very good at talking to large groups of people, and these were not going to be happy with him at all. Not one bit. He'd kept so much from them. And by the same token, he'd learned so much from them. They filed into the command center, and he was surprised to see that Ann and Margarita joined them. When they were settled, he began.

"I wanted to say how sorry I am." No one said anything, so he continued. "When I started this, with Rembrandt working with us, I had no idea that it would come to this."

"Come to what?" Hector looked at Skylar when she spoke up. "You knew even then that there was going to be an issue with these things. So what else did you think it would come to?"

"Ward and Dolin betraying me, for starters. When we first started this…when we all started this project, it was in our head…my head that we were helping this realm. The stones that we sought after were plentiful then. Or at least I'd been led to believe they were. And when we sent the first few malefactors here — as helpers, not destroyers — we thought that we were doing the right thing. I did anyway. I never realized how wrong I could have been." Hector turned and brought up the computer images that he'd had when coming here. "This is our realm. As you can see, things are not that much different from what you have here. The plants are different somewhat. We can grow most of what you have here, but not all of what we grow can be used here. The houses are set up differently. There is one room per house, and everything is out in the open. Light from the sun shines in all the houses from the top as well as the sides, and we have servants, at least some do, that do most of the work for us for a good coin."

"What was the reason you made the malefactors in the first place?" The question from Davis was a good one, and one he had thought would be asked. Nodding, he brought up the pictures of the wars.

"We were a peaceful realm. Rarely did we ever go to war. In fact the last time, before the malefactors, had been so long ago that none of us could remember. We live to be thousands of years old on our realm. We die from only a few things, and it had come to the point where we were being slaughtered right in our beds by other beings that would sneak into our houses and kill us. Our kind, the people from our planet, had no idea how to fight. So we...I came up with a formula that would change their chemistry and make them not just aggressive, but without thought to what they were doing. Killing without any thought to who or what they were killing."

"You did." Even though it was put as a statement from Rembrandt, he nodded anyway. "And then you thought to send them here when you were finished. When you released these monsters on us, did you have a plan to kill them off? Or did you plan to kill us all instead?"

"Neither. When we sent them here, it was with orders to only engage with the enemy. We didn't...we only had one enemy, one force against us. We never took into account that you would be fighting against yourself. Or that the enemy today would be your ally tomorrow. It was...it wasn't something that occurred to me." He looked around the room before continuing. "Then there was...they began to fight the control we had over them. The plan to bring them home...to be destroyed by us was...it was taken out of my hands. By the time I figured out that it was going to be bad, the malefactors were so many that destroying them was nearly impossible."

"Ward and Dolin." Hector nodded at Jarvis. "They did something on their end, something to the malefactors, which took this control from you. I'm assuming that's why you're here working with us."

"I had suspected it...by the time I realized what they had done it was too late for me to control the situation. I tried. There were...I found a way to kill off many of them, the malefactors...change them in a way that no human would see their bodies. But that too was changed. I don't know how they managed it; neither Dolin nor Ward have that much knowledge of what is going on. But it happened, and since I have no idea how they did it, I cannot reverse it. But I did find that if a malefactor is returned to our realm, they do not survive. Daily I have been sending as many back as I can. But it is draining." Hector looked at Rembrandt. "Then there was you."

"Me?" The big man stood up, his wings spread wide. It was a stance he'd seen him use when he was upset or fighting. It was a proud moment for Hector to see it. Scary too, but he knew that he had to tell it all. "You changed me without my permission. Everyone here has been changed by you without their consent. Why?"

"Because you are good men. Better men than anyone on this planet." He brought up the pictures of the other men, the ones that would join them. "Leonard has joined us, of course, but Leo did things for his students that no one else would. Giving them money when they had none for food or books. Class trips were often paid for by him. Coats were purchased with his—"

"That does not make me a good man. It makes me human."

Hector smiled and moved to the next picture. "Christopher Alexander. A man of all men. He is an honest man in a place where honesty is not common. When he said that he would help, he did. When things were down and nearly broken, he would rally all his men, who looked up to him, to bring things back to a place where they needed to be." Hector looked at the picture as he continued, "And never once did his name or picture grace the papers. He never took the credit where it was so richly deserved."

"And these men? Why did they not turn into what the malefactors are? Are you saying it was because of our hearts? That because we did what was needed and not what was expected of us, that made us not change?" Hector nodded at Leo. "I don't believe that. There had to be more than that."

"There is. There was. You were all dying, and had no one left to grieve for you." The next picture flashed on the wall behind him. "Richard Harmon was harder to find. He had…he had taken it upon himself to hide from all that were there to help him. Had I not…he was ready to take his own life when I found him. And when he gets here you should know that his chip is larger than that of Leonard. This man will be harder to convince that he is needed than even Rembrandt, with all his pain, was to bring over. Then there is Nathaniel Livingston. A man...Nathaniel, like the rest of you, was not human when I found him. He is a shifter with some special abilities. The man will bring it all together when he comes to his own."

"Who are the rest of them?" Vicki asked him as she stood up, her wings just as dark and spread as Rembrandt's had been. "I was told there were twelve of us. Twelve men to take this war on and win. Who are the other six men?"

"I never said they were men. I only...you believe that they are coming? More men are coming to join you?" She nodded. "I assure you that your combined powers, none of which I have given you, will be more than enough to take care of the malefactors. But you must come to your own."

"Six men. Just six of them are going to be victorious in all this? You expect six men, all of which have their own burden to bear, will be able to help in all of this?" Ann stood up as she continued. "I'm sorry, Mr. Hector, but I just don't see that it could happen. No offense to the rest of them, but they don't seem to know what they're doing most of the time. I've heard them say so. And to have them come here, mostly against their will and with nothing more than the little magic you give them, is not going to work."

"It's their mates." Everyone looked at him. "You...you will each have a mate to bring you to your own. A woman that will not just be...Rembrandt? Are you not stronger for having Skylar in your life? And you, Davis, since Vicki came to you, have you not...evolved as well? I will tell you that I had no idea that it would be as such. I assumed...I really assumed that they would be there for you to help you, but not on the scale that they have. And your new powers? I've been as amazed with them as you. None of what has happened since then has been anything that any of us have thought of. Nothing that I could have ever hoped for, but you have it all and then some."

"You're saying that because of our mates, the way that they...I don't know, complete us in some way...this is going to make us stronger?" Hector nodded at Leo, smiling. "Well, I guess we'll be one man out. I have no desire to have a mate in my life. I've been down that road, and it's one that I will never travel again."

Leonard got up and left the room. No one said anything for several minutes, and all Hector could think about was the poor man. He had really lost more than the rest of them. It was...he looked at Rembrandt when he cleared his throat.

"What do we do about Dolin and Ward? I'm assuming that by now they have gotten our message. I don't understand the reference to the turquoise, but I'm assuming you do. We use it, yes. It cuts through a malefactor better than a blade without it. And we know that that will go a long way to keeping us safe." Hector smiled widely and nodded. "I would like to know. I have...over the years I've figured out that the stone hold properties that kill the malefactors quickly, as I've said, but there is more I think. Much more that you've not told us. In fact, before we came in here, I put in an order for a large shipment of it. When it arrives, I plan to make small pellets of them and use them in our guns. But what did it have to do with Ward and Dolin?"

"It will kill us. Not quickly, as it does the malefactors." He pointed to a picture of Ward's home. "I have been going back and forth between the two worlds for weeks now. Setting up little things to make them think that someone is out for them. Not a lot of things, just moving things around. They are nothing if not paranoid. And I look for my notes. One of them has them. But the turquoise is part of the plan in that I put it on their person when I can, using the same principle that I did when I didn't want humans seeing the monsters get in and out of their houses. But when I find my notes, all my books, I'll be able to work out something that will destroy them all. I just need to find them first."

"So you're fucking with them." Not a term he was comfortable with, but he nodded at Jarvis, who in turn laughed. "Good for you. And so you know, if you want me to help you, I don't know, put in some cameras so you can keep an eye on them, I'm your man. I did that sort of thing all the time for a few banks and offices in the area. You'd be surprised what people will do when they think no one is watching them. I could tell you things that would—"

"Don't. Please." Ann stood up when she cautioned Jarvis. "Dinner will be in one hour. I have all the information that I need. But…I would like to say thank you to all of you. Had it not been for you all, I would be dead now. Not just the incident in the kitchen the other day, but with all of it. My daughter would have been…I just wanted to thank you all."

She left before anyone could say anything to her, and Margarita left a few minutes later. The rest of them continued to ask questions, but none of them brought up Leonard. Hector wanted to go to the man, comfort him in some way. But he was sure, like he'd been when he'd saved Leonard for this, he'd be pushed away once again.

Leonard was a man that was hurting more than he'd thought. The woman—her name eluded him now—had done a grand job of making the young man distrust everyone, and especially women. Leo needed his mate, whoever she was, to make him whole again. But if he pushed her away, Hector feared for the man's sanity. He surely did.

Chapter 10

Vicki, using her sword, cut through five more malefactors. Either she was getting much better at this or they were becoming stupider. She thought it was a little of both. As the last three were dispatched, she stepped over them to find Davis. He had gone in the opposite direction when she'd come to this part of the building. Vicki stopped moving when she heard the voices.

"I'm telling you as soon as I can find her, I'm gonna bring her to you. You won't believe all the shit she can do." Her brother. Pressing her body against the wall, she waited to see what else he had to say before she finally killed him. But the other person spoke first.

"I've no need for her. It's you I wish to recruit. There are things that I can do to you that will amaze and astound you." Randall asked if the women would like it. "Yes. I suppose they will. You'll be much bigger, more muscle. I do believe the women of this realm will enjoy that."

"Fucking fantastic." Vicki started to show herself, but Davis came into her view. His finger to his lips had her shaking her head, but her brother spoke again. "When do you do this shit? Today? I'm so ready."

"Yes, today. I will only need to do a few things to you before we set out." When Davis nodded, she moved out of the shadows. He stayed behind and it made her feel good to know she had backup.

"Don't do it, Randall." She looked at the man. "Which one are you, Dolin or Ward? I'm assuming you're here to change Randall into something more than he is now."

"Neither, as a matter of fact. I only work for them. You must be the sister. He never told me that you were a warrior." He looked at Randall. "How misinformed I've been. Why did you not mention that she was part of Rembrandt's little army against us? Had I known that, things would have been...well, no matter now, I guess."

"Rembrandt? You mean like the president?" Vicki rolled her eyes and said painter. "Whatever. I don't know him or what kind of army he has. But she can do shit with her mind that will make you a millionaire in no time."

"I've no need for money. Not any longer. But to have one of the warriors would make me a very high placed man in the new realm. Very high indeed." He took a step toward her, and Vicki drew her sword. "There is no need for you to get nasty with me. I'm much stronger than you are any day of the week. But you will bow to my superior strength soon enough, woman, and then you'll see what great things we have planned."

"Leave my brother alone, whatever you are. He's not worth you getting your ass killed over." Randall told her to shut up. "Randall, listen to me. You have no idea what this bastard has in mind for you to do. You'll be a monster."

"Sounds like a plan to me."

She looked at her brother and missed the movement of the man standing next to him. The long blade came out and was in Randall's chest before she could react. Then he was gone. The little man was smiling at her even as Davis came to stand next to her.

"You will come with me as well." He put out his hand as if she were really going to comply with him. "Come now and I will not harm your mate. I swear to you. You must trust me when I tell you it will be for your own good."

"I fucking don't think so. You killed my brother." The man denied it. "I saw you. You stabbed him in the chest and killed him."

"It is necessary for me to have given him near death to make this work. You will see once you are in the next realm. Glorious things are going to happen, and you will be a part of it as well. Now come along with me." The step he took toward her had her raising her hands. "There is no reason for you to fight this. You will only injure yourself, and I will have to explain that to my master. And if you are injured, he will be most unhappy with me. Thrilled that I have you, but unhappy because I've had to harm you."

"Your master can go fuck himself." That confused him, and while he was trying to figure that out, she hit him with a blast of her magic. He staggered back but didn't incinerate like the others had.

"You are no match for me, warrior." He hit her with something powerful, and it took her breath away. Davis held her, his arms wrapped tightly around her or she might have fallen. "Come to me now, or I shall hurt you again."

"Together."

She looked up at Davis; her body was drained of everything, and she wasn't sure she had much left in her. But when he put out his arm, the tatted one, she did the same. The surge of power ran over her, and she felt like she could do anything. Pointing her hand at the man, she was happy to see the look of fear in his face. Before he could do much more than utter the word no, they blasted him.

He didn't die. The man did, however, shift and change. His body no longer looked even like a human, but a...well, she thought he looked lizard-like. Davis pulled out his cell phone and began taking pictures. He was still taking them when the creature seemed to curl into himself and disappear.

Vicki felt herself being lowered to the floor. Her body felt like it had been sucked dry and only the shell was left. Davis sat down next to her and played on his phone while she rested. All she could think about was her brother. And if he was really going to be changed, she had a whole new set of shit to think about.

"He was such an asshole. He was from the first moment I saw him, until...well, forever." Davis asked her who. "Randall. All the time we were growing up he was the same. But when he hit about twelve he got into smoking pot, and then that progressed into heavier, stronger stuff. By the time I was in high school, he'd dropped out and become a dealer. By then Dad was gone and it was just me and Mom."

"Did he spend any time in prison?" She told him he had. "I thought so. He has the look of a man who has done time. I'm assuming that he wasn't in long. Or if he was, it was not as bad on him as it should have been."

"Five years the first time, then more the second. I lost track after that. What with going to school and working, I just sort of left him alone. Then Mom got to where she could no longer pay the bills, not and have him robbing her all the time. She said she didn't even know he was doing it until he'd already emptied her accounts and charged up her cards. He did that in less than two weeks. Christ, it was horrible." Vicki sat up, feeling better already. "Then he started hitting me up for money, which I had none. I could have given him a couple of bucks and that would have been stretching it, but nothing more. I was paying student loans, paying on a car he'd wrecked, as well as trying to help Mom with all the debt he'd put her in. That was when the beatings started."

"He should have had his ass kicked long ago. Was he like your father?" She nodded. "I'm sorry for that. Children are all we have to leave behind to remember us well, and most of the time...most of the kids I worked with didn't have a clue who their father was. I always thought perhaps that was a good thing for most of them."

"I knew my stepfather. Not well, but I knew him. He would knock my mom around, then get pissy when she had to spend time laid up. Or if she was in the hospital, he'd call me to come home and care for him. Like that was going to fucking happen. And he wasn't any better than Randall." She smiled at him when Davis stood up. "We're leaving? Something happen?"

"I sent those pictures to Hector and the rest of the command center. They want us back now. I guess we've given them things that Hector thinks will help us a great deal. Oh, and did you know that we're going to a party tonight?" She shook her head. "It's little Reuben's surprise. I'm not sure what that means, but he wants his family there. And that would include us."

As they made their way out of the building and into the dark night, she noticed that there were no others around. Not a single malefactor. Surely they hadn't killed them all?

But when a man stepped from the shadows, she drew her gun and pointed it at him.

"I want to help. We want to help you with this battle." She didn't move and neither did Davis. She did notice that Remy was coming up to the man's right and Skylar to the left. The man came more into the light, as if he knew he was making them nervous. "I'm from the other realm, the one where Hector and the monsters are from. There are...there are many of us that would help you. We've been...they think us all dead, and we have nowhere to go right now."

"How many of you are there?" She didn't look at Remy when he asked. His voice was hard and very unforgiving. "And what the fuck are you doing walking around a place where you might get your ass killed? You have to know what's going on around here if you've come to help us. You can't be that stupid."

"I'm not. I'm just a man who needed to provide for my family." The man pulled a box from behind him. "I worked for Dolin in the labs for a time. Until I saw what he was about. He's...you have to believe me when I tell you, those men are evil. This belongs to Hector. I took it before I left, and I'd like for you to give it to him. If you trust me after this, then I'll be back here in two days."

"And what if that's something we don't want to open? What if it's full of something that will harm us all?" The man knelt down and opened the box at Skylar's question. Nothing seemed to be moving out of it, and he reached in. "Stop right there."

She moved closer to the man and looked inside the box. When she nodded, he took out a large thick notebook and laid it on the ground. No one touched it, but it didn't look all that dangerous to her.

"It's his notes on the lab experiences. Dolin thinks he has them. But I had my daughter, who is seven, write in her best penmanship a bunch of things that she's taken from other books and magazines. It no more makes sense than us having to die for them." He stood up and backed from the box. "There are over two hundred of us here now. And more arriving daily. We have to go slowly, bringing over only five or six at a time. We can't be caught doing it or it's certain death to those we would leave behind. Like I said, they think we're dying off, and we want to keep it that way."

"Are you dying?" Vicki watched the man's face when she asked. There was pain there and a great deal of it. "How many have you lost? In your family...how many of your family have you lost to this madness?"

"My wife, a daughter, and one son. I have a son with me, but he'd been ill and I feared him dying before we could make the trip. But since coming here, all of us are getting better. I think—we all think—that we're being poisoned for some reason. In that box is a list. I got it from Ward's house. It's a list of the people that we think are going to serve them. The ones that haven't been sick or have lost any family members. They are not with us because we weren't sure if we could trust them." The man looked at Remy. "You're the leader. We've heard so much about you. Hardly any of it good coming from them, but we're...we want to help. We're able to help you."

Remy looked at them. It was one of the things she liked most about him...he never made a decision that would involve them all without talking it over. Vicki nodded once, then Skylar. Vicki could only assume that Davis nodded because Remy looked at the man.

"Your name?" The man told him. "All right, Hank. I'll be back in two nights at this time to talk to you if Hector says it's all right."

The man nodded. When he looked behind him, Vicki did as well. There was a boy there, small and weak, hanging on the arm of someone else. She just knew it was his son and that he was worried about his dad.

"I would request one thing." Remy didn't say anything, and the man smiled. "If you can see your way to knock out the other machines, I'd be very grateful. It's draining us as well as the monsters. We'll get stronger faster without them."

"Others? You know where they are?" Hank nodded and told him that there were seven of them total. He knew where they were because he'd been on the crew that set them up.

After getting directions to where they were, Remy and the rest of them watched the man slide back into the shadows. If he was nearby, they couldn't tell. And Vicki wasn't sure if that was a good thing or not. They made their way to the open parking lot.

"I'm going back through the air." Vicki nodded at Remy when he spoke. "I would like to suggest that we all go back that way. If the man is having us followed, we know it will be next to impossible for him to track us. The car will lead him right to us."

"Good idea." She nodded when Davis spoke. "I sent some pictures ahead too, as you know. Hopefully we can get some answers then. I think that Randall is going to be the next big weapon they put against us. I'm thinking that...they took him to the other realm for a reason. I think they plan to change him into whatever Benton is...or was."

Davis

Vicki spread her wings when they did and only hesitated for a minute to leave. Hank, with the young boy at his side, came out of the shadows to watch her. She turned to look at him when he didn't speak.

"If this is a trick, I will hunt you down and kill you." He promised her that it wasn't. "Remy and the others are good men. I won't let you drag them into anything. We'll help you if we can but not at the risk of being hurt ourselves. We'll kill you all if it comes to that."

"I swear to you this this not a trick. We're in need of help and we want to help you. If we can stay here after this is over, then that would be good too, but we can't go back so long as Ward and Dolin are there. They'll slaughter us." He looked at the boy, then at her again. "If he doesn't believe it's me or the stuff in the box, tell him January seventh. Tell him the date and that I said I'm still feeling it."

She nodded and took to the sky. As she landed on the ground near the house, she saw that Davis had waited. Leaning into him, she let him hold her.

"It's going to be all right. We're going to beat this. And we'll get your brother back. I'm not sure what sort of shape he'll be in, but we'll get him back as soon as we can arrange it." She looked up at him. "We have to do this if for no other reason than for your mom. She shouldn't have to know what he's going to do."

"He's dead. As far as Mom is concerned, he's dead. I don't want her to know that he's done this to himself. We'll tell her just what happened and that he's dead. All right?" He nodded and kissed her nose. "I love you. And I love my mom. And you're right, she would suffer, and I'd hate for her to think that he might be a monster that we have to kill sometime. And knowing Randall, that is just what we'll have to do to his dumb ass."

"And I love you. Very much. Let's get this meeting over with and then get to bed. I need to be inside of you in the worst sort of way." She took his hand and hurried him into the house. The sound of his laughter made her smile. He was the best thing that had ever happened to her.

~~~

They were getting nowhere with this. Not only that, but it seemed to Davis that they were going backwards. Hector kept saying they were his notes, but that he knew no one named Hank. Vicki leaned back, picking up one of the numerous notebooks.

"He said you might not remember him." Hector looked sad. And as much as he hated to admit it, Davis was disappointed that the man wasn't going to be helpful. "He told me just before I left that he was feeling it. I'm not sure what that means, and the date of January seventh. Does that help?"

It did. Hector paled considerably and fell into the chair behind him. Davis had a moment of worry that had it not been there, the man would have simply hit the floor. But as he and Vicki watched him, Hector looked at the notebooks again. This time Davis would bet he wasn't seeing them but the man and the day.

"I met my wife that day. She was coming out of a store or something and I saw her. A man was with her; they were laughing and talking to each other, and I could tell that it was...they had been dating for a while, it seemed. I didn't know his name for a long time, but he was her boyfriend and I guess lover. But when we saw each other, looked at each other from across the walk, I just knew that she was for me and she felt the same. She just walked away from him and came to stand by me, like she'd been waiting for me forever." Hector smiled sadly at the memory. "I found out later his name was Hank. And he'd been set to ask her to marry him that night, my wife had thought, and I had cut him off. I was that close to…I met him later. He was at a meeting with me. We talked for a while, then parted. I never thought of him since. But his parting words to me were 'I'm still feeling it. The pain of losing her to you, I'm still feeling it.'"

He stood up and set out the books. There were nine in all, and each of them were dated. Hector fussed with the books for ten minutes before he looked at them. Davis didn't like that smile.

"There is one missing. As it should be. The middle one. He'd not want me to have all of them should I not be here, or had I turned bad like the other two. If he was any kind of suspicious, he would have taken the first and last one too, but I'm glad that he didn't. I should like to work with him, if you are in agreement. He's a good man, smart, and he could go a long way into helping me find a cure for this to help what is left of the people here and us." Remy said that if he would work with Hank, then they would as well. "I thank you for that. He was…I think he was a chemist when he was with my wife. I do believe that he was fired at some point from the labs. It was about then that I was hired. If he's gone back to work for them, then there would be a good reason. He never trusted Ward. He told my wife once that if there was anyone as sneaky as he was, he didn't want to know them. For that alone, I think we can trust the man."

For the next several hours they all went over the books. Hector stayed at the huge chalk board that had been brought in for him, as that was what he preferred to work with, and wrote notes that he was taking from a book or two. As they each took a book and began reading passages, he made notes on them as well. When Remy declared that it was time to stop, the board and the tables were full of notes, note pads, and sticky notes. There was a wall of them as well, just a word or two here and there, and what looked like a formula written on something else. If it would hold ink, it seemed that Hector would write on it. And Hector seemed pleased.

"It really is too bad we cannot find him now. We're making such headway into this that his input would make it go quicker." Remy cautioned him about jumping in too fast. "I know, I know, but it has been so long since I've felt that I am being helpful. And productive. I have been nothing more than a burden since being here. I feel alive for the…you think me silly."

"No. I think you're excited. But we have as much to lose as we do gain if this is a trap. I know that he said the right things. But for all we know, he could have hurt the man who you knew to tell him that, and he is awaiting us to come to him. At this time of the game, we need to be on our toes. Not to say this man isn't what he says he is, but we have to be sure."

"But we're going?" Remy smiled at him and nodded. "Should we be afraid of you right now?"

"No, not you. But when we go, we go in force. We will not go alone, and we most certainly will not go unarmed. If it is a trap — and I'm not saying that it is, but if it is — then I would rather we be safe than sorry. Everyone will be ready to take to the skies. And those that cannot will be close to someone that can. We won't engage and hurt ourselves, but leave at once. They will expect us to fight back. We won't. I don't want us to do what is expected of us, ever. I think that's what has kept us alive all this time, or at least from getting badly hurt. I want to keep it that way too."

Davis was glad for the large dining room later that night. Everyone, including Remy, sat around the table and talked. There was no talk of the malefactors or the upcoming meeting. Dolin or Ward were not mentioned, and neither was Randall. It was what they all needed, and Davis was glad for them. It was like when they'd been in the yard and practicing their flying. It was just a group of people getting together. Of course, they were tatted up and had wings, and not to forget that they were going to live forever, but it had been normal and that was what they all needed a great deal of now.

"We should do this more often." Skylar laughed when someone said something back to her about needing to eat. "I mean, get together. And the fact that no one talked business was perfect. This room should be a safe zone. Never business in here. Ever. And we should be able to say or do what we want at the table. Like have a food fight should we want to."

"I agree." Remy stood up and held up his empty glass. "To my new friends and old ones. May we be friends for life, and our lives be longer than we hope. And I'd prefer that no food is thrown. I would have to explain to Ann why we tossed her no doubt delicious food around, and that would piss her off. Does anyone want to not eat? Yeah, I thought so. So no food fights."

"And to each of us, I hope for love. And happiness as long as we live. And that, my dear friends, will be forever, and I'm thrilled to have you all in my lives for that long." Davis added his glass to that of Skylar when she spoke.

"My grandmother was Irish, and she was forever quoting something. So this is for her." Davis cleared his throat. "'May love and laughter lighten your days and warm your heart and home. May good and faithful friends be yours, wherever you may roam. May peace and plenty bless your world with joy that long endures. May all life's passing seasons bring the best to you and yours.'"

Everyone cheered and sat back down. Remy stood up before speaking again. Whatever it was, he didn't look unhappy about it. When he looked around the table, Davis could see that he was emotional and that made him that way as well.

"On the day that Hector found me, I was ready to give up. I was...I was so close to death that I could feel it falling from me. I had lost so much, I thought. Too much for a single man to lose." He looked at Skylar. "And now I have a love that I cannot imagine being without, friends that make me strive to be the best daily. Pains in the ass that make me want to murder nearly hourly, but through it all, I have happiness where I never thought there would be any again. I want to thank you all."

"Who's the pain in the ass?" Davis laughed when Remy looked at Hector. The other man blustered for several seconds, then nodded. "Remy, you're a man of all men. A true friend and ally. One I am glad to call friend."

They went to the command center soon after and began working on the plans to meet Hank. Hector, with no sense of what might happen should they jump the gun, wanted to go now, but Davis and Remy, and even Leo and the others to some extent, could see the value in waiting. And planning. It would do none of them any good if they were to go in there half blind.

It was nearly four in the morning when they retired. Davis was exhausted, and Vicki was nearly staggering up the stairs, so much so that he picked her up and carried her the last few feet. He knew she was tired too when she didn't fuss at him. As soon as he put her on the bed, she rolled to her side and didn't move. Davis smiled while he took off her shoes and clothing. Crawling in beside her, he felt wonderful when she rolled into him and curled around him. This was something that Davis thought he could get very used to. Closing his eyes, he let sleep take him under as well.

Chapter 11

Vicki didn't like this. Not at all. It was too dark, and there were way too many things that someone could hide behind. She said as much to Remy, and he agreed. Then why, she wondered, were they still here? Hank was late. He was very late as far as she could tell.

The little boy came out of the shadows and didn't move. He didn't say anything either, which sort of creeped her out a bit. She'd been around Reuben long enough to know that they rarely, if ever, stayed still. And this kid was as still as the light pole he stood by.

Hector went out first. He was the one who would know the man, but since there wasn't one, she supposed it was still best for him to be the first. Vicki moved closer to the two of them, keeping an eye out for anything that might be dangerous. Like this entire thing wasn't already.

"Hello. I'm Hector. I was supposed to meet Hank here. Do you know him?" The boy did nothing. "What's your name?"

"He's dead." Vicki felt her breath whoosh from her lungs. The voice did not match the kid. It sounded like…like one of those creepy movie voices of the possessed guy. "One of the malefactors got him. My dad is dead because of you."

Hector nodded but didn't turn to look at any of them. It was his signal that he wanted the fuck out of there now. Instead, he got down on one knee and nodded to the kid.

"Do you know where he is now?" No answer. "He was supposed to meet me. He has something of mine. Do you know where it might be? If you'd let me, I'll have him buried in the way of our kind."

"Didn't you hear what I just said to you? He's dead. He's fucking dead. Don't you even care that he's gone because of you? You killed my daddy, and now I'm all alone." Vicki felt the hair on her arms rise. There was something so very wrong about all of this. She looked at Skylar when she moved up beside her.

"He's lying. And I know as well as Hector does that they cremate their dead, not bury them. He's trying to trick the kid up." Vicki wanted to ask her how she knew, but Skylar continued before she could. "He's not his son but something else. Someone else. Now we just have to figure out what he's doing and where Hank is."

Vicki closed her eyes. She'd met the man, Hank, and thought of him. Something had happened to her the other day, and she wondered if she could make it work on Hank and finding him now.

Two days ago, just after she and Davis had parted in the house, she'd wondered where he was and was surprised when she felt him…knew that he was in the kitchen talking to Remy about something. And when he looked around as if he'd known she was seeing him, she stopped, and ever since she'd been playing with the trick to do it where no one knew. While she wasn't perfect at it, she was getting a good deal more comfortable with using it.

"He's still at the place...a building with large windows and a green front door." Moving into the building, she could see him as clearly as if he were standing, or in this case sitting in front of her. "Someone has been beating him up. He's strapped to a chair by his arms and legs. Hank is awake, but he's pretending to be unconscious. His face is bloodied and his arm is broken. They want him to tell them where the book is. I can turn and see the man, but he's deep in the shadows right now. This kid is not his, as you said."

"Can you see the building again? Pull out or whatever you're doing and have a look at it." If Skylar was surprised by what she could do, she didn't act like it. "Maybe you can get a number. Something else to go on. Or even a street sign. Look around like you did inside the building. Tell me everything you can see."

Vicki moved out of the building; it was strange, but it was like she was floating around, not really walking. That was what had been the most fun in this new trick, moving like she was in a video game. It was a little disconcerting at first, but as she practiced, she got a lot better at that as well. The streets, of course, were dark, but there was a light near the end of the walk. Moving in that direction, she could see the street names, both of them.

"Main and Shipley. It's about five...six buildings up from the corner. Across the street from it are two cars, one of them a long stretch and the other...I'm not sure. Something old and beat up." Moving back into the building, she moved to each floor. "There are three floors. No one on the upper one, but there are two...no, three on the roof. They're armed with guns. Body armor too. I'm not sure what kind it is, but it's thick and dark."

"Good. We'll start there." She opened her eyes and looked at Skylar. "Well, who else would go? You have a birdseye view of the place, so it's not like we're going to get hurt. And the men can handle what's going on here. We'll be in and out while this is going on here. Hank will be saved, and we'll be all right with what you can do."

"But this kid? What do we do about him?" Remy slid up beside them and kissed Skylar and nodded. Then he looked at her and winked. "We're going alone? Do you think that's a good idea? I mean, we can do this, but what if something goes wrong?"

"Yes, we're going alone, but I'm not worried about it so long as you keep an eye out for the bad guys. And if we run into trouble, Remy or the others can be there in a few minutes. But you know that we're going to be fine." She moved back, and Vicki went with her. She wished now she'd just kept her mouth shut and her head where it belonged. Fuck, this was going to get them both hurt.

She and Skylar took to the skies. Vicki could take off well and could once in a while land well too, but she knew that as soon as she fell head over ass at the site, she was going to fuck them both up.

They landed on the street over from where they needed to be. She had thought they'd land on the building, take out the bad guys, and then go in and get Hank. But Skylar told her what if they got the wrong building? True. And when she didn't mention that she might land wrong, Vicki was ever so grateful. This was why she was a nurse and not a strategist.

When they found the right building, Skylar went first and then Vicki followed. As they both put their feet down on the building right behind the guys with huge fucking guns, Vicki took off the first man's head, then turned to the third man while Skylar killed her guy.

He was gone.

When he wrapped his arm around her neck, it was all she could do not to scream out in frustration. Skylar walked to both of them with the head of the guy she'd just killed still in her hand. After she lifted it up to make sure that the man saw it, Skylar tossed it behind her and lifted her sword again.

"You're going to die, you know that, right?" The man just laughed, and Vicki could smell his putrid breath and gagged. "If you let her go now, I'll just cut your fucking head off and not chop you to bits like I'm prone to do. I love it when a man is chopped up, don't you? Especially when you get to his tiny little dick. It just makes my day when I can cut it off, then using tweezers and a little knife, cut it into nice earrings for me." She winked at her.

"Yeah. Makes it easier to flush them too. However, his twig and berries you can leave alone. I can feel them, and they're not worth the bother. Not even for earrings." Skylar looked down at his waist, then frowned at them. "Trust me, not worth it at all."

"Fucking cunt. I'll show you just how fucking big I am." He shoved her away from him and started for his pants. Skylar had his head off before he even got the button on his jeans open. For several seconds the women stared at each other, then burst out laughing.

"If he was the smartest one of the group, we're not going to have any trouble. Men and their dicks...what is the big deal?"

They went to the door through the roof and moved down the stairs by flying down them so as not to make any noise. They were at the door when Skylar pointed to her eyes and then the door. Nodding, Vicki looked into the room with her special magic and could see it perfectly. She had noticed that the closer she was to where she looked, the better it was…the clearer, she supposed.

Five men. She put up her fingers to show Skylar, then touched Skylar's arm to point to where they are. When Skylar stiffened, Vicki realized that she could see the room as Vicki was. Fuck, this shit was amazing. Vicki took her around the room with her. It was wide open, but there were large poles between them and Hank.

"We go in quick and kill fast. No fucking around this time." Vicki wanted to point out that she'd not done the fucking around, the shit hole had, but nodded when she smiled. "Kill and move. Okay?"

Kill and move. She made it sound like she was telling her to pick an apple and eat it. But Vicki knew she was right. There were more of them than the two of them, and they had to hurry so they'd not get the chance to kill poor Hank while they were trying to get to him. As soon as the door opened, the hinges not making a single sound, they both hit the room flying.

It was over before she had thought it would be. All five men were dead, their heads laying a few feet from their bodies, and she and Skylar were standing in front of Hank. Skylar pulled out her phone and sent a text message. It simply said, "Done." She knew that as soon as they got it on their end that things would go differently than the bad guys had hoped. They cut Hank loose, and Skylar picked him up when it looked as if he wasn't going to be able to stand on his own.

The clinic wasn't far away, and they took him there. As Skylar laid him on one of the gurneys, Vicki dressed to help. She had on her gloves just as Weston came into the room. Her mom was right behind him. This was going to go quickly.

He had three broken ribs, with lacerations to his face and chest. All of them required stitching up, so her mom did that while they worked on setting the rest of his wounds to rights. His left eye was swollen shut, and there was some bleeding from his ear that concerned Weston. It was several hours before they were ready to go back to the place where the boy was. But Remy texted and told them to wait.

"What's going on?" Skylar shrugged. "Could it be a trick? I mean, that kid wasn't human—could he have hurt one of them, taken the phone, and is messaging you?"

"You do have a vivid imagination, don't you? No, I don't think any of that, but thanks for planting it in my head." Skylar looked at the sky, then back at her. "I suppose we should just go and check. Not get into it, but just do a fly by and see."

She was all for that. As they took to the air, Vicki felt somewhat better about this. Not great, but better about being close. And as they neared the area, she could see that things were not as good as she and Skylar had had it.

~~~

Remy saw them above. Christ, this was out of hand. He was fighting for all he was worth, and it wasn't nearly enough. Whoever this thing was, and he had no doubt that it wasn't human, it had an army of things like him. The same creature that Davis had taken pictures of the other day was now overrunning them, and it wasn't going to go well.

The kid had morphed. Hector had backed away once it was established that the kid wasn't going to be helpful or forthcoming, and that pissed it off. His body changed so quickly, had Remy not been standing close to Hector, he might have gotten seriously hurt. As it was, the man was down and out, but was protected by them as best they could. Whatever these things were, they really wanted Hector.

The first blast of magic hit two of the creatures. He knew it was Vicki and was glad that they'd come back. Long ago he'd lost his phone in the fray, and now he wished that he and Skylar had another way to communicate. When her voice, suddenly sounding terrified, spoke right behind him, he nearly got himself stabbed looking.

I'm not behind you but over across.... How the hell am I talking to you? Remy looked up. *There is some weird shit going on. You should see what Vicki can do with her mind. And she can share it. Mother goose balls, we're an odd lot of beings.*

Mother goose balls? You know what, I don't care where you got that. Have her kill this fucking bastard in front of me and I'll gladly let her show me what she can do. He laughed when the monster suddenly disappeared in a blast of light. *Thank her for me. And where is Hank? You didn't bring him here, did you?*

No, he's in the clinic. I told...where is your phone? He told her he didn't know. *Someone messaged me with it. If Vicki hadn't gotten all paranoid, we'd still be back at the clinic awaiting your okay to come here.*

I'm glad. I'll thank both of you a great deal later. Fuck, we're outnumbered. Help.

Skylar was suddenly right in front of him, and he used her like he'd done before, by pulling her body to his and putting their tats together to make a clean sweep of the things as they grew in number.

He hated to bring Skylar into this. More than anything, he didn't want her hurt. But between him and Davis flying down and taking the monsters out by dropping them on the ground, they were going to need the extra help or they'd be dead by now. He'd not been able to leave Hector, and Davis was doing the best he could keeping the things from overpowering him. Leo was working at the other end, where the things were coming from, and he had no idea if the man had been hurt or not. Remy hadn't seen him in ten minutes or more.

Within minutes of the women showing up, things were nearly manageable. Davis was pulling a body from in front of the door to one of the buildings, and Vicki was picking them up and dropping them several hundred feet to their deaths. Her magic was draining, he knew, so he wasn't surprised to see her use it only when necessary. Davis made his way to her, and they, too, used their combined power to kill the bastards. As soon as the last monster was dead, Remy sat on the ground.

"What the fuck are those?" No one answered him, and he really hadn't expected them to. Hector had told them it was a form of guard for the royal family, but they'd been dead. The monsters had been killed off for decades. "Who the hell is bringing them back? And why would they? I mean, for us I guess, but then what?"

"I would say that it is Ward and Dolin, but you more than likely knew that. I'm not sure how they're doing it, but they are replicating them at an alarming rate." Remy wanted to point out that he could see that, but didn't think Hector would understand. Vicki was looking over the man's arm as he continued. "They take several generations to mature into what we're seeing here. And trust me, I would have noticed these things moving around the grounds. They're messing with their DNA, and if that's true, they have no idea what might happen should they ever reach the age where they are controllable. They'll be…they're going to be the death of my world, I think."

"Why?" Hector only looked around for an answer that he didn't think he had for Leo when he asked him. "I mean, I understand why they've done it. To kill us off, but why? I was sure that they're doing enough damage with just the malefactors. Why would they need more things to take over? Not just for us, surely?"

"Perhaps they sent them here only to kill us. Or me. I would have…should I have been alone, I would have died. Or been taken. As it is now, we're outnumbered but not out…what is it you are saying all the time, Remy?"

"We're outnumbered by not outgunned." Hector smiled and told him that was right. "But these things, they're not like the malefactors. They're more…I want to say deadly, but that's not quite right either. It's as if they're more single minded, like focused on getting you. That was their objective, and killing us was just necessary."

"That is what they were to do when we had them. Kill a certain being or get a thing that might be on another planet. Once they had it, or the person was dead, then they were as docile as a kitten but with sharper teeth." Remy nodded at Hector's explanation. But it still scared the shit out of him to know that there might be more of these things, and that those two might be trying to think of bigger and meaner things to kill them with.

Davis sat down beside him, as did Leo. Remy was glad now that he'd left both Jarvis and Jake back at the compound. They would have been more in the way than helpful. Even with them being shifters, they were still likely to have been killed.

The clean-up was nearly done when Remy realized that he should have been helping. But he was tired. As the last of the creatures was disposed of, he stood up. Walking around the area, he began to pick up the stones. There were twenty-three of them in all.

"If you don't mind, I'm going to go and see that those machines we were told about are taken care of. I'm not sure how, but I'd just feel better knowing." Remy told Davis to take Vicki. After a few minutes, Leo drove Hector to the clinic, so it was just him and Skylar.

"You all right?" He nodded at her but walked around again. He thought he'd gotten them all but wanted to make sure. These things could be dangerous if they fell into the wrong hands, and he wasn't willing to knowingly put things out there that they could use. "Remy?"

When he turned, she was naked. Her wings were the only backdrop to her otherwise gorgeous body. Tossing the bag of stones in the general direction of the tree she was near, he willed his own clothing away and moved toward her. His cock was so hard that he was sure he was going to hurt himself.

"You are beautiful." Nodding, she dropped to her knees in front of him and took him into her mouth. His half-baked plans to take her against the tree vanished as soon as she cupped his balls in her warm hand. "Christ, yes."

There was no foreplay needed between the two of them. Their entire day was one kind of sexual pass or another. She'd flash him her bare breasts, he'd cup her ass. Every time they were together, even with others in the room, they would touch each other, fondle something until they were sure of getting caught. And when they came together, like they were now, they were both so needy that the thought of foreplay would have been a waste.

When she cupped his balls, rolled them in her hands again, Remy curled his fingers into her hair and held her to him. He was fucking her mouth hard when she dug her fingers into his ass muscles, and he nearly cried out with the pleasure of it. She looked up at him at one point, and he could see that she was enjoying herself as much as he was. Her fingers at her breast made him want to take her right then and there.

He felt her swallow him down. Over and over, her mouth opened around him, and Remy could see her slick saliva all over his cock. As she fisted him, licking her tongue around the crown of his cock, Remy pulled her up by her hair and kissed her. He needed her, but this was not the way.

Lifting her up, he took her to the tree. It wasn't just a need to be inside of her, but an all-out necessity. As soon as she wrapped her legs around him, Remy slammed his cock into her heat and pressed her against the tree all in the same motion. Christ, she was so wet, her heat seemed to consume him. Remy gentled his taking her enough to look down at her.

"I love you." She nodded and licked his throat. "You bite me now, and I won't be able to hold back from coming in you."

"That's the plan." Her teeth scraped none too gently over his pounding pulse. Tilting his head, he offered her his throat and anything else she wanted. As soon as she bit him, sank her teeth into his neck hard, he came, pounding into her like he was driving a nail. He felt his balls fill almost as soon as he emptied them.

His second climax took his breath away. She screamed around his flesh as she too released. Remy nuzzled into her throat the moment she sealed the wound at his neck and bit her hard. Her hot blood, spiced with her need, seemed to pour over his body and into each organ he had. There was nothing about this woman that he didn't love. Inside and out, she was his. And Remy realized right then that he was hers too.

Drinking greedily, he fucked her through two more hard climaxes before he lifted his head to look at her again. She was more than just beautiful; she was far and away the most wonderful creature in the world. Any world. Remy held her to him as her body, still coming and tightening around him, settled. There would never be a time that he didn't enjoy her coming down as much as he did building her up. When she went limp in his arms, he knew it was time they got back. They were alone and it was dark.

Dressing quickly with clothing that he thought up, he kept touching her. It was as if he couldn't get enough of her. When she came to him, the bag in her hand, he pulled her into his arms and kissed her until he had to lift his head to breathe. She was smiling at him.

"We should get home." Nodding, he didn't let her go. "Someone might come looking for us. What will you tell them delayed us?"

"That I needed a good fuck and you were here." She smacked him on the arm, and he let her go. "Should I tell them that I simply needed the loving of a good woman instead?"

"No. You should just keep your mouth shut before this good woman gets pissy and takes your twig and berries off you." He asked her what that was, and she pointed to his dick. "I heard Vicki call them that tonight. She's a hoot, did you know that?"

"I'm beginning to think that the two of you would be better off not hanging out together. You're too…dangerous alone. The two of you together could cause a lot of damage to someone." He laughed when she did. "I like her. She's good for Davis."

The area was as clean as they were going to get it. The blood, like the malefactor blood, wasn't visible to humans, but he knew that it was to the monsters. While they might not know what happened, they'd know that a great many of their kind had died there. Thank goodness they hadn't encountered any humans in all this. There was enough blood here now that it looked as if someone had murdered several hundred people. As they moved to the skies, he thought about all the things they'd discovered tonight, and asked Skylar about what else Vicki could do.

"Vicki can see beyond where she is. She needs to only think of a person, like she did with Hank, to see not just where he was but the men that were with him." She told him what they had done. "And when she touched my arm, it was as if I were there with her. I could not just see what she could, but could talk to her as well so that we could move around and have a good plan."

"That is very…we'll be using that a lot, I think. Do you think that Davis can do it too?" Skylar told him she would imagine. "Maybe she can…I don't know, pass it on to us. Or perhaps it might be one of those things that makes them special from us. Christ, I wish there was a book or something."

"Yes. It would be nice, but I'd not count on that if I were you. But I have to tell you, it was as if I was snapped into a video with her. She told me later it was much like a game she played once in a while. She called it a third person shooter game. I'm sure that her mind is using that knowledge to make it work." Remy could see that. Use what you know, he'd always said. "She said that the closer she is to what she needs to see, the clearer it becomes. I'm just wondering now if she can see into the other realm."

"We'll have to test that out when we get a minute. That would be a good tool in all sorts of things that might come up...not just with the malefactors, but all kinds of things." They would need to make a list soon, he thought, of all the things that they were figuring out and who could do what. "How about you being able to talk to me? How did you make that work?"

"I didn't. You did. I felt it in your mind that we should be able to talk to each other without using devices that can be broken or lost." They landed in the yard as she continued. "It's a good thing and safer too. I told you that we got a text from you, telling us to not just stand down but to wait for you. I don't even want to think about what might have happened if we'd have done that. Hopefully the rest of them will be able to communicate with us this way too. I can see where that would be a safe and quiet way to talk."

The kitchen was empty when they entered. There wasn't any cause for alarm, but after tonight he was a little on the stressed side. Voices from down the hall toward the front of the house had them going in that direction. Everyone, including Hank, was sitting around the television watching a movie. Remy stared at the screen for several minutes before he realized they were watching a horror film. He thought they'd all gone off their rocker after what they'd just seen when one of them spoke from behind him.

"It's not all that scary now." Remy looked at Leo when he spoke, handing a large bowl of popcorn to Ann and Margarita. "After tonight...well, this is sort of tame, don't you think? I mean, we've killed nastier things than this has in it. We've been giving commentary on it, sort of screaming at the screen when someone does something incredibly stupid. They do that a lot in horror films. Did you know that?"

Remy was handed a bowl of popcorn, and before he could think that he shouldn't, he cupped a handful to his mouth. Remy moaned at the taste and ate two more handfuls as he made his way to the couch. Christ, it was like manna.

"I made it with my special recipe." He wanted to jerk the bowl back from Ann when she took it from him. "I'm only going to refill it, Remy. I'll give it right back."

"It's the first popcorn I've had in...." He smiled. "I've never had popcorn before. I had no idea I could even enjoy it. And whatever you put in that stuff, I like it. No, I love it. Can I have my own, please?"

When she returned a few minutes later with two big bowls, he took one and handed the second one to Hector. He was nearly done with it when he finally asked Ann how she'd made it. He stared at her as she explained.

"I make my own caramel, then pour it over the popped corn as I bake it in the oven. I've been making it for years." He asked her how to make the caramel. "Oh, that's a snap. I take some cheap sweetened condensed milk and simmer it in a pot of water for two hours. Less if I want it creamier or longer if I plan to make caramel balls with it. Then I roast some pecans and put them in the popcorn as I roast it. What you're eating is the last for tonight."

"I want this every night." She laughed, and he frowned. "I'm not kidding. This is the best dessert I've ever had. And I want to try your caramel balls too. Dipped in chocolate. Can you do that? Oh and I'd like some chocolate dipped pretzels. I loved chocolate when I was human. We didn't get it much because it was expensive, but I really liked it. Dark and rich."

"Yes, I can. I can also make caramel turtles if you'd like. Chocolate chip cookies with or without nuts. " Remy asked what a caramel turtle was. "I put pecans in a circle, then put a dollop of caramel on it. After it cools enough to handle, I dip the entire thing in chocolate. It's really very high in carbs, but very delicious."

"Whatever you want, I will get it for you. Just promise me that you'll make me something like this every night." She told him she would make whatever he wanted. "I don't know what I want. This is the first food I've had in…much too long to remember. Please? I'm begging you. I want some sweets. And chocolate. Don't forget the chocolate. I'll order some for you. We'll…we can try all kinds of it."

"All right. I bet you don't even have to worry about getting fat either." Remy shook his head. "Lucky man. I need only to look at sweet stuff and I'm as big as a house. I'll have to make better use of the gym. Not that it would hurt me anyway. But I'll make you things and you can figure out what you want. But not just sweets. You have to have a balanced meal too."

Remy finished off his entire bowl and was eyeing the other one when Skylar sat on his lap. She turned his head to look at her, and he wanted to growl.

"Don't be a pig." He tried to pull from her grip, and she jerked his head back. "Seriously, you've eaten more than your share. It's rude to take everyone else's treats. You're a grown man; act like it and not a little spoiled baby."

"It's very good. Have you tried it?" He reached into his bowl only to come up empty handed. "Let me get you some from the other —"

"Behave." He realized then that he was being childish. But who knew that something as mundane as corn could be so amazingly delicious? Certainly not him. He wondered aloud how many other things he'd been missing and started to get up. "If you as much as look in the direction of the kitchen, I'm going to brain you. Ann would go with you and cook you something, and she's exhausted."

He looked at the woman sitting in the chair across from him. She did look tired. And he realized how much she was doing around here. Cooking for all of them, all the meals whenever they needed to eat, cleaning up after them and helping in the clinic when she could. Remy looked at Skylar.

"We need to get her some help. Fast." She nodded. "But who and where? I mean, it's not like we can just hire anyone off the streets to come into his house. We're not exactly human here."

"I've been thinking that too. I had hoped that the people that came from the other world would be able to help out, but I just don't know who to trust. I mean, tonight we were nearly taken in by a kid." He nodded and pulled her closer on his lap. "Who do we find to help us?"

"I can help." They both looked at Hank. He looked bad, too bad to be sitting in a chair, but Remy had been told he'd insisted on being up and about. Ann said he was trustworthy and even Skylar said she could trust him. "I have...those others that I told you about. They're needing to do something. Most of us are domestic help. All actually. But there are a few that can...we were pressed into domestic services as the ones that the richer people employed started to die or leave. I'm sure you can get as many of them as you want to come and work here."

"How do we know who can be trusted so we're not taken in again by a child?" Hector cleared his throat as he joined the conversation. "And so you know, little Sam is bunking with Reuben. I think they're getting along very well."

Remy had forgotten about Hank's son. The little boy had been rescued right before he and Skylar had come home. He'd been beaten up a little, but not like his dad, and was more than likely as well as he was because he'd escaped on his own. It had taken Leo an hour or so to get him to come with him. Trust, it seemed, wasn't just as issue with them.

"They won't be able to get past the barriers." Remy looked around the room at the group there. "We'll be safe so long as they can get by the barriers. Those that don't...we'll deal with that when we get there. But I'd really like for Ann to have help as soon as possible. Please give us a list of names that can help and we'll get started on that tomorrow."

Hank said he would and asked for some paper. The sooner the better he said when told it could wait until tomorrow. Things were beginning to come together, and Remy was as much afraid of that as he was relieved.

Chapter 12

They began to arrive at sunrise. There were twenty at first. Most of them were nervous. Hell, so was she, but Vicki had said she'd help interview them, and that's what she'd do. But now it was nearly noon and she was hungry and tired. The woman who had been hired as a second cook sat a large bowl of soup and a sandwich in front of her before walking away with a short nod. Vicki looked to see that Ann and her mom had one as well.

"You should eat before it gets cold." Vicki nodded at the woman she'd been interviewing. "I know Lana. She can make the best soup you'll ever eat. And her pies are to die for. She used to have her own little shop until someone with money decided that they wanted her to cook for them. She had to close it up. The rest of us were sorely disappointed."

The soup was amazing. Not normally a vegetable soup fan to begin with, this made her want to have it every meal. And the sandwich tasted like the bread had been freshly made, and the meats were so juicy and tender that it nearly melted in her mouth. She finished it off before she thought about how she must have looked.

"I'm so sorry." The woman laughed. "I never eat like this in front of someone. You know, like a starved animal on their first meal in ages. But you're right, it was the best soup I've ever eaten."

"It's fine. She is that good. Lana can also make bread and cookies that will make you beg." Nodding, she picked up her pen and looked at the list of things she was supposed to ask. Instead she looked at the woman.

"What is it you want to do? Not what you did before you were taken into household cleaning, but what do you want to do?" The woman looked shocked, then nodded. "You weren't always kitchen help, were you? Tell me what you did before some asshole decided you needed to make his bed for him."

"Thank you. I was…believe it or not, I was in charge of security. I could…I kept the higher-ups safe from all kinds of issues. Not just on the ground, but in the air as well. Our first attack all those years ago came from the sky. It was me who alerted them that we had incoming. Then about a month after they started making those things, I lost my job, my house, as well as my husband. He was pressed into becoming one of them." She looked ready to cry. "I will do anything. I don't care for being idle at all. And I know that humans for the most part do not hire women to be in charge of things like that, but as I said, I'll do anything for a steady income. Most of us have nothing left, and it will be hard to start again, I know, but I'm willing and able."

Vicki wrote on the sheet what she thought the woman was suited for and sent her to see Jake. The man was just as exhausted as the rest of the household was after all this. Perhaps the man could use the help or not, but she was betting he'd take her on. The next few people who sat in front of her she did the same thing, asking what they wanted rather than what they did in the other world. She was writing yard work on the top of this person's personal sheet when Ann sat next to her.

"I have a request." She nodded. There was little that she'd not do for this woman. "I need someone to be able to bake. Someone to do the shopping as well as put things away. A dishwasher would be nice too. One that will wash as I make the mess and not say a word about how many pans I use." Vicki was making notes as someone sat in the chair. The person looked at the list and raised his hand. He took the sheet from her and began writing. Vicki looked at Ann, who shrugged, then at the man. When he finished, he handed the note to her.

"'I cannot talk. It is a birth defect. I should very much like to keep the kitchen clean.'" She handed the note to Ann. Standing, she motioned for the man to follow her, and he turned and waved at her. That was easy, she thought with a laugh.

The rest of the day was just as easy. Of the hundred that had shown up, they had hired them all. And tomorrow looked to be just as promising. In addition to the ones that now worked at the house and the grounds, a lot of them were working at the clinic downtown, as well as the newly acquired apartment building that would house them all. Remy was looking into buying two more buildings when Davis told him to hold off.

"We need the room. There are any number of people living on the grounds now that have nothing more than a tent to live in." Davis nodded and started to speak when Remy cut him off. "I know what you're going to say. I'm jumping into this too fast, but winter is coming and I don't want anyone to suffer."

"Right. But that wasn't it." Vicki laughed, and they both glared at her. "I was going to say that I'd like for you to buy the entire block. There are five apartment buildings in that area. And since the humans are all…there is no one living in anything there any longer. They're furnished and have power for now, but we'll have to figure that out too. And there is a grocery store close by that needs some care. You know, take the bodies out that are cluttering things up. I was thinking that we could hire a few men and women to run that as well as…I'm thinking outside the box here."

Remy nodded and suggested that they have a garden. A large one to help with the food costs. Davis sat down and started making a list of things that had to be taken care of in the future, like the garden and what they'd need get it started as well.

"Oh." Vicki flushed when they both looked at her. "I forgot about…most of those people would have left things going on. I mean, food in the refrigerator. Alarms going off that no one is there to hear. They're all gone. I know that I should have realized it before, but it just hit me, no one is there."

Davis held her hand while she tried to regain control over her emotions. She knew it was because she was so tired, but with this help—and there was a lot of it—maybe they'd be able to rest better knowing they were getting it all done instead of doing only what needed to be done .

"We'll need a clean-up crew for all the buildings." Remy started to make notes too. "We should also find out if anyone can go to the power plant. There has to be someone there to see that we continue to have heat and light."

"And the schools. There are a lot of kids here now."
Remy nodded at her suggestion. "Someone will need to
take over those as well. I'm sure that there are a few that
can lend a hand in that department, as well as a bigger
clinic. Christ, this is like we're starting over with
everything, isn't it?"

Vicki looked at Remy's notes. She noticed that his
handwriting was very floral, very beautiful script. Then it
occurred to her just how old he was, and how much he'd
seen and done in all his life. Nearly two thousand years of
just living and killing. Her heart broke for him too. The man
had lost a great deal, more than anyone else had.

"Remy?" He looked at her when she didn't continue. "I
wanted to say thank you. I would be dead by now had you
not...had you not been what you are."

"Thank you too, love." He looked at her for several
seconds before he bent his head to the task. His voice was
filled with humor as he continued. "But you're not getting
out of some of this work. There is more here than I first
thought. I know nothing of running any of these things."

As so for the next several hours the five of them, Skylar
and Leo included, went over things that they might need to
do. Who knew that starting from scratch—and that was
what they were doing—could be so much work?

~~~

Dolin sat in his chair, not moving. Something was
going on here. Something scary. He watched everything
within his vision. Someone was messing with them and he
was terrified about it. The fucking stone was appearing in
the most...he'd taken to having all his pockets sewn shut.
Dolin had locked doors to his house, the inside of his house,
to keep the intruder out. Nothing was working. The brisk
knock at his door had him cry out in fear.

He got up to see who was at the door, careful nowadays to see that no one came in that had not been invited…which was most people. There was Ward and a woman who brought his food to him, but she wasn't allowed beyond the garage. A garage that was empty of everything he had owned. Getting rid of it had seemed so important at the time. Now…well, now he had no clue why he'd given away his car, his lawn mower, as well as his lawn furniture. Not that he'd ever sit out in the yard again until he figured this out, but it was devoid of everything.

"I've been trying to reach you." Dolin nodded and was tempted to pat his friend down. "I've been reaching out to your buddy, the one that was on earth, and there is no answer. So I went there. He's dead. All of them are."

"What do you mean, they're all dead? That's not even possible. They're our creations, and no matter what we put at them, nothing killed them. Do you know how hard it was for me to figure out how to resurrect those things? And to make it so they'd grow much faster than they had before?" Then something he said occurred to him. "You went there? You went to earth? Why? How? When was this?"

"I didn't actually go there, but visited. You should see the mess left behind. I have no idea what killed them, but there are body parts all over the place. And there wasn't a single stone to be found anywhere." Dolin staggered back from Ward. This was all just too much. They were being conspired against, and he had no idea why.

And there were so few people here now that even his list of names wasn't all that helpful to him. There had to be an end to this soon. If not then they were set to lose it all. He moved to his chair, looking to where the stone was he'd put in the glass container an hour ago, and noticed that it was gone again. There were no pockets on his clothing…he'd taken them off the last time he'd found it on him. Dolin found it in his underwear this time while he was patting himself down. Jerking his clothing off, Dolin stood there naked with the thing in his hand, sobbing.

"I can't get rid of it. I buried it the other day. Deep in a hole that took me hours to dig. When I got home, it was sitting on my table covered in dirt and waiting for me. I don't know what to do."

He sounded insane. Dolin knew it. And he was beginning to feel like it too. And from the look on Ward's face, he was thinking he was too.

"You need to calm down. I don't know what you're talking about. And please, will you just stop crying like a child? You're not making any sense right now. Take a deep breath and let it out—"

"Look. Do you have the stone on you? Your stone? Do you have it?" Ward nodded with a leery look on his face. "Is it turning up all over your house? I mean even on your person?"

"Yes. But I'm ignoring it. You seem…are you unwell?" He wanted to scream at him that he was just fine. It was the stone that was all wrong. "Give it to me. Once I have it in my possession, you won't have to worry about it again. I'll take it home and put it with mine. That way you can not worry about it again."

"Yes." He reached out to hand him the stone, and Ward just looked at him. It was then that Dolin realized he was naked, with a stone in his hand that he'd just taken from his under clothing. "I'll just get dressed and wash this up as well."

"Please do." Dolin wanted to snarl at Ward that he was too fucking calm to suit him. But he only walked to his room and put the stone on the dresser. It would have sounded insane. And he wasn't. Dolin was a brilliant man, and this was just…it was just too much.

As he dressed, never taking his eyes off the stone for more than a second or two, he felt reasonably better when it was still sitting where he'd put it to begin with. Taking it out to Ward after washing it and his hands, the man put it in his pocket. He did feel calmer now. The thing would be gone and he'd not have to worry about it.

"I'm sorry. You have no idea how this thing has been ruling my life. It's like I can't get rid of it. And it's making me ill as well." He showed Ward his legs and the bloodied streaks that had formed earlier today. "I'm not well when that thing is around, and the stress of having to keep up with it is making the illness worse. I know that in my head, but I just can't deal with it."

Ward took the stone out of his pocket and stared at it for several seconds. Then he asked for a plastic bag. After putting the stone in the bag then taking it to his car, they sat down in his living room. Dolin asked Ward what he'd been saying when he first came in.

"We sent down fifty-five. All of them we had, remember? I knew we should have kept one of them to study if needed." Ward paced around the room twice before sitting down again. "There is something else. The ambush didn't work, as I said, but they found out about the other…about Hank. They knew where he was, like someone told them just where he was. All those men? They're dead as well. And they have the book, I'm assuming."

"The ambush was supposed to rid us of all of them at one time. You assured me that they'd all go together to protect each other." Ward nodded and looked so depressed that Dolin didn't want to be mad, but damn it all to hell.

"The kid, you said it would work too. They'd never guess it wasn't a kid, you said to me over and over. Now look. We've lost an entire army of beings that I don't know if I can make again. What happened to the kid-like being? I mean, are they so far gone that they'd kill a kid? I need answers, Ward. They're not playing right. They're just being mean now, don't you think?"

"I don't know; it does seem as if they're just out for blood. I don't understand it. We're the superior race here, not them. They should have just given up months ago and let us have what we wanted. But they keep…they killed all our beings. As well as the ones that we had holding Hank. How the hell did they know about him? Who is giving them this information? We can't find a single person to go into their house and kill them all. And until that brother is finished with his training and change-over, we're without any other means to show them that we mean business. They have not just infiltrated our work, but have killed our best men."

Dolin had no idea. But someone was helping them. These people were not this smart. He and Ward were well beyond their intelligence and everyone knew it.

"How is Randall coming along anyway?" Dolin only shook his head at that. It had been a major disappointment as well using this man. "He still complaining about everything?"

From the first moment he'd opened his eyes, he'd done nothing but bitch and moan. He wanted more drugs. There were too many people around him all the time. The clock was too noisy. Dolin had been so stunned to hear that complaint that he'd gone to ask the man about it.

"Could you please explain to me how the clock could be too loud? I've never…not in all my years as a lab tech have I ever heard such a complaint. Do you have, perhaps, better hearing than most?" He hadn't meant to sound so...snotty, the man had called him, but it was a good question.

"The constant tick-tock, tick-tock is just going on and on. Can't you hear it?" He could and started to point out that was the way clocks worked, but Randall continued. "Turn it down or I'm out of here."

"There is no way for you to get out of here, Mr. Randall. Should you do that, you'd surely die when you crossed back over the realms. It is all that is keeping you alive, you being here until this change is complete. And it is not complete, not at all, and leaving now would make it so we'd have to start all over in the process. We would very much like to have this done and soon. We have money riding on this. Rembrandt and the others will surely —"

"You lied to me then." Dolin was shaking his head as the man tried to get from his cage. It had become necessary to cage him days before when he'd become too much for the lab technicians to handle. His temper was worse than a rabid animal that had been cornered. "I want to leave here now. I want out of this cage and out of this place."

They'd drugged him then, and he'd been that way since. Dolin had never figured out the clock and didn't bring it up again. He had, however, had it removed from the room and put somewhere else. He realized he'd not answered Ward and mentally shook himself to remember what it was they'd been talking about.

"Randall?" Ward nodded. "I have not been down there since we've had to keep him sedated. The man is coming along well, I've been told. Just a few more weeks and he'll be ready to unleash on the other realm. They will not have a clue that he's part of our team and not with them, as he'd been all along. His sister, we're hoping, will welcome him into the house with open arms. Then it will be easy from there."

"Nothing about this has been easy. And nothing has gone even close to the way we had hoped it would. The only thing that has gone right so far is the death of Hector's wife. The rest has been nothing but a disaster." Dolin could agree on that. "I just hope Randall is as able to talk to his sister as he says. I just...I've begun not to trust anything with this."

"As much as I hate to admit it, so have I. I think the man is a pain in the ass, and there is no way that he will be as much help to us as we'd been told. There is something so very wrong about him. I wish now that I could contact the man that we sent to get him. There has been no word from him...he was my first attempt at the creatures that we sent to earth. I was fond of the man. And now...well, now I fear that he is dead as well." Each of the men in the lab had told him and Ward several times that Randall had the ability to do great things, if and only if they were able to finish what they'd started. But no one, not one of them, would say for sure what his greatness would be. Only that he was going to be that. Dolin thought perhaps they were lying as well, just to make them look good in light of what the man was doing.

As they talked about the issues that they'd run into, not complaining but going over them one by one and of course blaming Hector for each of them, Ward's phone went off. He got up to go to the other side of the room after looking at it. It was more than likely the lab. Days ago, when it became apparent that someone was coming into his house, Dolin had refused to leave his house. Now they were instructed to call Ward instead of him. When he came back,

Ward sat on the couch again and Dolin knew that something was wrong.

"He's gotten away." Dolin was afraid to ask who because he was pretty sure he knew. "Randall got out of his cage and destroyed most of the work that had been started on him. Killed four of the men working there, as well as the guard at the door. They—whoever is left—are out looking for him. But him killing those men, the ones that worked for us? We have no one to replace them, Dolin. We're going to have to do something soon, or we will be the only people left here and no one to rule. I want to rule, damn it."

As did Dolin. He was almost embarrassed to think about the scepter that he'd bought a few months ago, and the beautiful crown that he'd commissioned to have made for him. It was bejeweled and made of the best gold. There had been several smaller agates that he'd put on it that had since been taken out to use for their work. Yes, Dolin thought, he wanted to rule more subjects than just Ward. He looked at the worried look on Ward's face and nearly just asked him to go home.

"There's more, isn't there?" Ward nodded his head. "Tell me. I'm sure I don't want to know, but you have to tell me. If not, I will worry about it for days until you come back here and tell me anyway."

"He's taken all the magic we had in the building. And he's…he's taken it." Dolin asked him what he was talking about, his temper no longer easy going with this thing. When Ward, usually a strong man—stronger than him anyway—burst into tears, Dolin felt his own fill his eyes.

"Taken it as in he's now holding all the power that we had? Everything that was in the building? He has taken it into his body? Tell me." Ward sobbed more, and Dolin was on his last bit of patience when he finally looked at him.

"Randall is now...Christ, he's the strongest thing ever to come from here. Ever. Do you have any idea what that means?" Dolin did but said nothing. "He can destroy us. He can...he will harm us, and we've done nothing wrong. We just wanted them gone so that we could be rich and this is how...they're not playing fairly, Dolin. Not fairly at all."

"We have to plan. We must hide now." Dolin stood up. "I have my shelter. We'll go there. Everything we need for years is there. I have it ready. There is food and money there, as well as water. There is...you must come with me now. We're in danger."

He didn't tell his friend that in the last week he'd been stocking more things than was necessary down there. More food stuffs than he could eat in a year's time; more than enough time, he thought, for things to be back to normal. There were batteries enough to fill a large room. All of it had been delivered to the garage over time and taken down by himself. Dolin had wanted to move down there without the fear of the stone. Now...well, he'd have to make room for Ward now. He supposed he could just send him home and move in without telling him, but he would be lonely and he needed someone to talk to.

"Now?"

Dolin grabbed up the pillows from the couch. He was headed to the door when the first pounding came. Ward stood there staring at the door as the wood began to splinter, and the man on the other side began to taunt them.

"Dolin, my man? Wardy, my buddy dear? Are you in there? I need to speak to you." It was Randall, and he was talking to them in a singsong voice that made the hair on the back of Dolin's neck dance and tingle. "Dolin? Answer me, you cock sucker. I want you to see what I've done to myself."

189

The voice had changed now. Slurred words made him think that the man was inebriated, or full of drugs. Dolin had an idea that was just it. Not the kind that he'd been taking on earth, but the kind that would make him into a monster. He'd be bigger now, stronger than he'd been before. And they had no way of knowing what sort of magic he'd have. Dolin had been mixing things together for days before leaving the lab for good. If he had even a tenth of Dolin's creations, Randall would be something horrific to see.

"Hurry." Dolin finally had to grab Ward's arm and drag him behind him as Randall continued talking to them. "The door won't hold much longer. And if he gets in here while we're up here, he's going to kill us both. You have to hurry or I shall leave you here, Ward. Come with me now or face him alone."

Ward nodded and started after him. The door to the front of his house shattered just as they rounded the corner to get to the shelter. Dolin was running now, dragging his friend for all he was worth. They weren't going to make it, he kept telling himself. They were going to die, and that would be horribly unfair. Running faster when he heard nails, like those of a large cat, on the floor in the other part of the house, Dolin pressed the necessary buttons to have the door opened.

The door to his shelter opened with a small puff of air. Stepping into the shaft, a smallish elevator really, it was closing when he saw the creature that they'd made. Good Christ, it was worse than he'd thought. The man was more than a monster, but several of them at once.

The doors closed just as the creature saw them. His claws scraped across the steel of the door just as it was closing. Dolin was sure he'd never forget the look of it for as long as he lived when the thing—Randall—threw back his head and roared. The elevator moved to the lower levels, and above them they could hear the house being destroyed. Dolin was sure that things were not going to be the same when he got to go back above ground.

"Oh my goodness. Oh my goodness. He nearly got us." Dolin only nodded, his own fear making it hard for him to breathe, much less speak. "That thing...that monster. What are we going to do with it? Surely he'll...what are we going to do now?"

"Live here. We can for as long as we need to." Ward looked around as Dolin continued. Dolin looked at his shelter through Ward's eyes as he exited with him from the elevator.

"This is...you've been very busy getting ready for this, haven't you?" Dolin told him he had. In truth, while the shelter itself had been there, he'd never done a thing to prepare it until the stone started to move about. "We can live here, you think? Stay down here until the monster up there is gone?"

"I didn't want to be caught unawares. And stocking this place gave me something to do when I was grieving for my Mary." A lie again, but Ward patted him on the back as if he knew what he meant. He hadn't wanted to be killed was what it was. "I've been expecting something like this. Not Randall, but an uprising. I didn't want either of us to be hurt when it came right down to it."

When he'd been filling the shelter with things lately, he'd never thought of anyone being with him. Ward was his friend, his best friend actually, and he was glad now that he'd been here when it became necessary to use it. His plan, if he ever really had one, was to use this for him and Mary if needed. But she was gone now, thanks to those people. They had so much to answer for, and he was going to make sure that they did. Dolin looked at Ward when he realized he'd been speaking to him. Asking him to repeat it, Dolin felt embarrassed.

"And all this. How did you manage it?" Ward waved his hand over the green house he'd put in. It was huge, and the plants he'd started a few weeks ago to keep himself from starving were coming along nicely, if he did say so himself. "You've been preparing for this to come soon?"

"Yes and no. I've been...I wanted to be eating better and this was here. I thought to myself that I could get the hang of it where no one would be able to see that I'd failed should I not be a good farmer." Partly true. He did want to eat better, but the rest was a lie. "You should see the rest of the place before we begin working around things."

"Whatever will I do for clothing?" Good question. All the clothing that was here was mostly for him. But he took Ward to the second bedroom and showed him the clothing that was stored there. "I could wear these. They'll be a little snug, I think. You never were good at guessing my size. Remember the sweater you gave me several years ago? I still laugh about how large it was on me."

Dolin nodded. He'd not guessed at his size at all, but he was all right with Ward thinking that he had. And the sweater he'd given him had actually been a gift from someone else to him. Dolin hated sweaters, and when Ward had shown up with a gift for him, it had been easy to give him that one. The thing had still been in the box and had a bow on it.

"You have a look around. If you have any questions, I'm going to be monitoring the outside world with my system." Dolin had been quite proud of himself for thinking of that. If the world, their world, went to shit, he wanted to have a first-hand view of it. He never expected that they'd be the cause of the world falling apart, but it wasn't just his fault. It was Hector's and Rembrandt's. Had they just…well, he was sick of saying it, even to himself. As he entered his little office, he realized that Ward had followed him.

It took him several moments to get the hang of the controls. He'd been playing with them, of course, but the cameras that he'd had installed all those years ago had been replaced in recent years, and he still had to think before moving them. One such move nearly made him throw up; it was like being on a boat with rough waters. When he finally got it to move in the right directions, he found his home…or what was left of it.

The house—his house—looked like someone had taken a large wrecking ball to it. His little garden was gone, covered in debris from the patio surrounding it. The windows, all of them, were broken out and glass was everywhere. He had to think where his door had been because of the destruction that had occurred. Even his garage, although it was empty, looked bad. Dolin just stared at it, thinking how he could have been there among the rubble.

They looked at the town in general. The only place that had been destroyed was his home. Ward had asked to see his, but there was not enough range for him to do that, and Ward said that he thought perhaps his would be fine. Dolin was doubtful that things were ever going to be fine again, but said nothing. It was going to be a long year if he had to keep biting his tongue this way.

Chapter 13

Leo was in the middle of his exercise when he felt it. He wasn't sure what it was, but the rumble in his body made him think that someone was giving him more magic than he'd had before. He was going to be pissed if they did that again. As far as he was concerned, he had all he could handle right now. When nothing more happened, he went back to lifting the barbells that he was using.

The pain was there. Not like before, but he still hurt from the things she'd said to him before she'd tossed the ring he'd given her on his lap. CarolAnn Rivas had been his one and only true love. She'd been his world.

"I'm not going to be able to handle this, Leonard." She would never call him Leo, no matter how much he'd asked her to. "I know that if we were married now, I'd pretty much have to stay at your side, but we're not and I'm really glad that we found out now."

"Found out what? What are you not going to be able to handle? The job? I assure you that once I'm gone, you'll have enough to not work again. I have...." She was shaking her head at him. "Then what is it?"

"You." He had still been confused. "I looked it up, you know, what I was going to have to go through once you were really sick. Christ, couldn't you have gotten something that would have been easier to handle?"

"The next time I get a fatal disease, I'll see if they'll give me something that will make me go quicker for you." He was joking, sort of, but she was nodding. "CarolAnn, I was joking. You do know that I have no control over what I have? That I was sick more than likely with this for a long time before they found it."

"That's what I'm trying to tell you. It was as if someone didn't think we should get married." He shook his head, more out of disbelief than that he didn't understand. "Don't tell me no, Leonard. I've been thinking about this a lot. And you're going to be dead soon. Why should I have to wait and suffer too?"

"Yes, we can't have you suffering, now can we?" He was hurt and his temper seemed to show it. But she only kissed him on the nose and stood up. "CarolAnn, we're supposed to get married in a few weeks. What the hell am I supposed to tell people? That you didn't want to be with a dying man?"

"Of course not. Do you want them to think that I'm callus?" He wanted to point out that that was just what she was, but she continued before he could. "I'll just tell people that you decided that things were going to be too hard on me, and you told me you didn't want to bring me down. It's not like you're going to be around long to tell them any different anyway. And once you're dead...you don't have to change your insurance policy, do you?"

"I don't have to, but I will." She asked him why. It wasn't as if he had anyone to leave his money to. "I would rather leave it to a man on the street than to let you have a dime of it."

"Now you're just being mean. I've done nothing that any other woman of my station wouldn't have done too. You're just being cruel to take me out of the policy. That's a lot of money, and I have had to suffer taking you to the doctor that one time." He only stared at her as she continued berating him for his not taking care of her once he was dead. "I'll just have to talk to a lawyer, I guess. Once you're dead, I won't—"

"Will you stop saying that?" CarolAnn backed away from him when he stood up. He hadn't been weak then, not like he was a few days later, but it had caused him to lose his temper. "Get out. Get out of my place and don't you dare return."

Two days later, he'd gotten a letter from her attorney telling him that he wasn't able to take her name off the policy. Which, he supposed, was fine by him, as he'd never put her on it anyway. Leo had been meaning to. For several days it had been on the top of his list of things to do, but he'd put it off. And right then, he was glad that he had.

Leo didn't even bother replying to the firm. He was finished with them anyway. He was dying, and soon. When he'd gone to the doctor, the one and only time that CarolAnn had taken him, he'd been told that he had less than a month to live. That the cancer had taken over and he was lucky to be up and around now. The day after the letter came, he'd been put in the hospital when he'd passed out at the grocery store. The next day, the man in black—Hector, he knew now—had come to see him.

"I have a job for you." Leo had laughed. He was well beyond working at anything other than staying alive. "You will have more power than you've ever had, and you will work harder than you ever did at teaching."

"I don't know if you've been told, but I have only a few days, less really, to live." Hector had only nodded. "I'd really like it if you got the fuck out of here, buddy. If CarolAnn sent you, tell her to fuck off too. I'm as good as dead."

"You'll work with a brilliant man. He is very...old, I would say, but he is a good man." Leo didn't bother answering him. His body was used up, just lying there. "You're going to be well, never to be sick again. Your life will be long; forever, should you choose."

"CarolAnn would hate that." Hector asked him who that was. "The woman that was supposed to be with me until death we do part. Or until I do the death thing and she takes my insurance money and runs. Just go away. I'm very tired."

"Leo, you should know that once you die, I cannot bring you back. You'll have to agree to help us now, while there is still time." Leo had told him again to fuck off, but he was falling into the tar of darkness again and wasn't sure that he'd answered him.

The pain in his arm made him look at Hector. He was touching the place where the IV was feeding into his arm, and the burn made him think that the man had given him something to make his death quicker. Right then Leo didn't care, and closed his eyes again. It was then that he saw the dragon.

He was huge, and his wings made him thing of King Arthur's Court and the Knights of the Round Table...swords and magic, as well as damsels in distress, and hot sweaty nights being thanked by the same woman.

The dragon seemed to know him, he remembered thinking. It spoke to him, breathing fire over his body and telling him that he'd be fine in the morning. At the time, Leo thought it was the burn from whatever Hector had been giving him and he wanted to say that. But the dragon continued to tell him that he'd care for him, and Leo wanted to believe him. Still did as a matter of fact.

When he opened his eyes, he'd been alone in the dark room. There were noises going on down the hall, an intercom telling them that there was a code in room nine sixty-four. Leo had lain there, listening to the machines at his back and sides make their sounds. The squeak, squeak of shoes on the floors as someone went by his room, and he felt…well, he felt really good.

Leo had thought for sure that he'd died. That this good feeling he was having wasn't because he was better, but because as a dead person there was no more pain. He was only lying there until someone, or even something, came to take him away. But when the nurse came in to take his vitals just as the sun was cresting his window, he asked her if she could see him.

"Of course I can see you, Mr. Earl. You have some color in your cheeks, and your lips are not as dry. You're using that stuff like I told you, aren't you?" Leo watched her as she took his blood pressure and his temp. She took it a second, then a third time before she went out and came back again. "There was something wrong with that one. It said you were off the chart."

He put the thermometer under his tongue this time. The one that had touched his forehead was laying on his bed. When the alarm went off that signaled that the reading was finished, she stared at him, then at the machine. He asked her what it said.

"That your temp is one hundred and forty-seven and rising." He knew that the regular temp should have been less than one hundred, but she didn't seem to be overly concerned, so he didn't worry either. "They're coming to draw some of your blood soon, so you'll have to wait on your breakfast. It's still only liquids, but I can get you some more juice if you want it."

Leo had been starved. Not hungry, but actually starved. Like he'd not eaten...well, he'd not eaten in two days, and now he wanted it all. He asked her if he could have something more, and she only shook her head at him. When the nurse came in to take his blood, he'd been ready to steal the candy bar that he could see in her lab coat.

The doctors had come and gone before he got up. He was stronger too. His body felt like he could lift a car. When he was alone in his room, he'd lifted the chair and then the little dresser. Before he was finished, he'd put the dresser on the chair and lifted it. Leo had never ever felt this great. And that feeling had nearly gotten him put away. Smiling, he thought of the doctor that he'd lifted up with one hand when he tried to tell Leo that he was too weak to be released.

"Good memories?" Leo turned to look at Vicki when she spoke. "You were smiling. I assumed you were having good memories."

"I was." Getting up from the bench, he realized that he'd been lifting weights for nearly two hours and he was sore. "Did you want something from me?"

Leo knew that he'd made a mistake the moment she stood up. Vicki was one of the nicest people that he knew, but she was very touchy about things. And she was mean when she was pissed off. Bracing himself for whatever she might blast at him, he was surprised when she turned and left him. And for some reason, it hurt him a great deal.

~~~

Master moved about his cave. He wasn't getting any better, and he was reasonably sure that he was dying. The stones had been used up almost the first hour of him returning to his new home, and now he had nothing. Also, when he tried to reach Dolin or Ward, he hit nothing but a hard wall.

The fire blazed hot, but he was still so very cold. He had no idea what kept the flame running all the time without wood, but he assumed it was magic. It was why he'd picked this particular cave. There had been a hum about it that he'd not been able to ignore. Looking down at his abused body, he sobbed again.

"Why? Why did they do this to me?" Master no longer blamed the women. Nor did he even think that Rembrandt had anything to do with what was going on now. Sure, they'd harmed him, but they'd not forsaken him. Dolin and Ward had done that to him. They'd promised him so much and had left him to die.

Master moved to the fire, close enough that he could feel the little sparks of it touching his skin. His body, no longer able to shift, was weakening daily. He knew that it wasn't just a matter of if he was going to die, but when. Whatever he'd been hit with, it had been pure and it had entered his heart and damaged it. Taking away the cloth that was as much a part of his clothing as his pants or shirt, he looked at the wound.

It was a gaping hole. Ragged, of course, but he could see his ribs that held his chest together, as well as a part of his lung that had also been affected. The blackened part that was showing smelled pretty bad now, but there was little he could do with it. But his heart was what had been hurt the worst.

The place where his stone had been was now a cavity. When he'd first made it back to the cave, he'd shoved all but one of the stones he'd had left into himself to try and help. It had for a time, but that hadn't lasted long enough. The pain, the terrible overwhelming pain, brought him to his knees more and more daily. Master lay down on his pallet, unable to go to the bed that he'd had brought here so long ago.

"I should return to the other realm. If there, I know that I could heal myself. The magic there is—" The noise behind him made him curl tighter into a ball and lay still. Whatever was coming could kill him or not. There was no fight in him any longer.

"Benton?" He didn't know the voice, so he waited. "Benton? Come on out. I want you to show me how to use this fucking magic."

Magic? Master didn't move. He was terrified it was a trick. It would be like them, the blood brotherhood he'd been calling them because they were banded together like a group of vampires. When a shadow fell over him, he only looked up at the beast before whimpering.

"They did a job on you, didn't they?" The man or beast of a man was having trouble keeping his shape, changing from monster to man repeatedly. Master had to look away. The movement was making him ill. "You have to show me how to use this shit. I left before the lessons began."

"I don't have it in me to help you." The pinch of something in his leg had him lifting his head, but he felt the burning before he could ask what the man had done.

"That'll help you, I think. It sure did me." The needle was just being pulled from his body when Master felt himself…well, he was himself. His body felt energized; his heart started to pound in his chest. For the first time in days he could take a deep breath. And when he did, Master stood up. "There you go. Works better than a hit of coke. Christ, I feel fucking good when I take a hit of this shit."

Standing up, he let his beast take him. The amount of energy that he got from the simple shot was making him feel as if he could take on the world and win. Looking at the man/beast standing next to him, Master had the most uncontrollable urge to hug him, then rip his throat out. The rage that was slowly taking over his body was making him ill with it.

"What is that?" The man only shrugged. "You gave me something that you've no idea what it is? Are you insane?"

"You're not dying now, are you, fuck balls?" He had a point, but the rage, the anger was making him take a step toward him. "You try it and I won't ever give you any more of it."

That stopped him. "It's not forever?" The man shook his head and said it would only last about a day before he needed more. "How much do we have? Enough to live out a long time?"

"Nah. That's why I came looking for you. We need to find us somebody to make more of this shit. I took it to a friend of mine to have him brew it, but he was a little freaked out by me and I had to…well, he was screaming a lot and it hurt my head. That's something you should know, loud noises will set you off. And the feeling of being really fucking pissed all the time will make you kill for no reason. Not that that part bothers me much, but it's hard to get anyone to help you when you're raging on them all the time."

"How much? And where did you get this?" The man sat down. His body was calming now, but he still had no control. "Think of holding one or the other. You're making me sick. Just think of your body, the man inside of you, and hold him in your vision. That should do it."

It worked, and the man was so pleased that he smiled. Master backed away from him. His teeth were not like a humans, but sharp and dirty. Blood seemed to be staining them, and he was sure that there were...things hanging from them that he didn't want to know about.

"I got this shit at the lab. There's a little more but not a whole lot. I might have destroyed a lot of it before I left. They sort of pissed me off. Did you know that they locked me in a fucking cage?" Master told him he'd been there too. It was where he'd been made as well. He then asked him for his name. "Oh yeah, I'm Randall Carver. That asshole, Ward, kept calling me Randy like I was some sort of pervert or something. I'm going to kill that fucker when I see him again."

"Where is he now? And Dolin? Do you know where they might be? I have some things I'd like to go over with them too." Randall told him what he knew. "So they just disappeared, did they? I'm betting they made it to the hidey hole that Dolin has. He thinks nobody knows about it, but I have my spies."

Master had no such things, but he'd heard someone say that Dolin was setting up this place and bringing in a lot of supplies. He had no idea where he'd heard it or even when, but he knew that it had been recently. One of the men he'd contacted at the lab might have had it in his mind when Master had tried to find Dolin and had touched his mind.

They talked for another hour. Master had missed talking to someone that felt like he did. Others, most of the people in the lab and here, had thought that he was a monster. He was, but there was a difference in what he thought he was and what the public thought of him. By the time they were on their way back to the other realm, Master was devising his own plan to get more of the drug. And it didn't include the fool that was with him.

He had to tread slowly, however. Randall wouldn't say where the drugs were that he'd taken, nor would he tell him the dosage that he'd gotten. He did warn him that taking too much could really "fuck with your mind," whatever the hell that meant. Master thought that something had already fucked with this person's mind and he was going to have to kill him…and soon.

Things were starting to look up for Master, and soon he'd have Dolin and Ward where he wanted them. Then he'd take on Rembrandt and the Brotherhood.

About the Author

Kathi Barton, author of the bestselling series Force of Nature, lives in Nashport, Ohio with her husband Paul. In addition to writing full time Kathi likes to spend time with her eight grandkids, three children and three children-in-laws. She writes to relax and have fun.

Her muse, a cross between Jimmy Stewart and Hugh Jackman brings them to life for her readers in a way that has them coming back time and again for more. Her favorite genre is paranormal romance with a great deal of spice. You can visit Kathi on line and drop her an email if you'd like. She loves hearing from her fans. aaronskiss@gmail.com.

Follow Kathi on her blog:
http://kathisbartonauthor.blogspot.com/

The best way
to thank an Author
is to leave a
review

Now Available Book 1 in the Blood Brotherhood Series, Rembrandt

www.ingramcontent.com/pod-product-compliance
Lightning Source LLC
Chambersburg PA
CBHW032125170626
46808CB00006B/2108